BIKER

BAD BOYS IN BIG TROUBLE 1

FIONA ROARKE

BIKER
Bad Boys in Big Trouble 1

Copyright © 2016 Fiona Roarke

This book is a work of fiction. The characters, organizations, events, and places portrayed in this book are products of the author's imagination and are either fictitious or are used fictitiously. Any similarity to a real person, living or dead is purely coincidental and not intended by the author.

Nickel Road Publishing
ISBN: 978-1-944312-01-5

Published in the United States of America

DEDICATION

For K, who nudged me, pushed me and then gave me a hard shove. For R, who provided the sweet beverages, including copious amounts of Kool-Aid. For L, who made lots of chocolate treats to get me through. And for JR, who inspires me and then promptly supports whatever I decide to do. Thank you all.

Despite the danger, there are some definite pluses to undercover agent Zak Langston's current alias as a mechanic slash low-life criminal. He doesn't have to shave regularly or keep his hair military short. He gets to ride a damn fine Harley. And then there's the sweet, sexy lady next door who likes to sneak peeks at his butt. Yeah, that was a major plus.

Kaitlin Price has had the worst luck with men. As if her unearned reputation as a frigid tease isn't enough, she also has to deal with her stepsister's casual cruelty and taunting tales of sexual conquests she can only dream of. So Kaitlin has never been with a man. So what? So what…

So maybe the sexy bad boy next door would be willing to help her with that.

Gunfire, gangsters and a kidnapping weren't part of her Deflower Kaitlin plan. Good thing for her bad boy Zak is very, very good. At *everything*.

Biker, Bad Boys in Big Trouble 1
Nothing's sexier than a good man gone bad boy.

PROLOGUE

Zak Langston pulled the single sheet of paper from the envelope and read out loud, "Assignment: Biker." There were more words below that, but the single-word title occupation made him stop reading.

"Biker? Really?" he asked his handler, Miles Turner. "You want me to join a gang or something this time?"

"Yes. That's exactly what we want you to do. We even have an initial contact to help you out. He's a mechanic at a garage in the small town where the bad guys are headquartered, and you're about to get a job there."

"He's an informant, then?"

"Not exactly."

"Explain."

"Your assignment is to infiltrate the gang with the help of a civilian we'll arrange for you to meet. Get in with them, set up a deal to stop the bad guy leader, and then come back for your next mission. Simple."

"It's never that simple."

"Of course not. So you'll adapt and overcome. That's your job."

He rolled his eyes. "Right. So where am I going?"

"Arizona."

"Awesome." His tone was anything but excited about his new assignment. "It's super-hot there."

Miles grinned. "But it's a dry heat."

"You're not helpful."

"It's not my job to be. Helpful is for Boy Scouts and brown-nosers." That was his handler's favorite phrase to quote, second only to his very favorite regarding promises.

"Anything else I need to know?"

"We found a place for you to live, but you'll have to sign a six-month lease."

"Six months! It won't take that long, will it?"

"Of course not, but the rent is so reasonable it's worth it. Plus, you'll be centrally located in town."

"Good enough. I'll be on my way then."

"Great." Turner's voice turned serious. "And Zak, take these guys seriously. They're more dangerous than they seem at first glance."

"No problem. I always take these guys seriously. Crazy not to."

"And stay in touch."

"I'll think about it." Zak typically maintained the absolute minimum amount of contact when he was undercover. The last thing he needed was to be caught with a bug in his ear or talking on the phone and having to pretend a meaningless conversation when someone walked in unexpectedly. "You'll hear from me when I have something relevant to report."

CHAPTER 1

The old saying about stopping to smell the roses was in Kaitlin Price's case better revised to halting everything to stare at her new neighbor's well-sculpted butt. She did this every single day when he returned home from work. He never disappointed.

Kaitlin was on a mission, and it most certainly involved Zak. As a bonus, he looked very much like a bad boy. Bad boys and the way they operated was perhaps a stereotype, but hopefully an accurate one. She didn't even know Zak's last name. Not yet. But she would. Soon. Or not. Didn't matter. She didn't need his last name for him to fulfill her most ardent wish.

She just hoped he'd be willing to cooperate with her seductive proposal. Stereotype or not, he would fit the bill perfectly where her needs were concerned. Plus, she *really* loved the view.

Like all known procrastinators, she'd waited until the last possible second to enact her "seduce the neighbor" plan, so basically it had come down to a now-or-never situation.

Her strategy *had to* be enacted tonight.

Tomorrow would be too late.

A familiar throaty roar echoed down the street, interrupting her mental schemes and sending her scurrying down the stairs to the side window in her living room, which had the very best view.

With a glance at the hall clock along the way across the room, Kaitlin pulled the curtain aside and peeked out as the sound of a loud motorcycle approached her home. The object of her desire came into view as his Harley turned into their shared driveway. He veered off the single rectangle of pavement slightly and onto the short sidewalk in front of his porch.

Zak.

The new bad-boy neighbor who'd moved in next door a couple of weeks ago.

Her landlady, Mrs. Waverly, owned not only Kaitlin's home, but also the house next door. Zak's house. When he'd signed the lease agreement last month, Mrs. Waverly had come straight over under the pretense of "informing" Kaitlin to expect a new tenant. She'd then proceeded to tell Kaitlin everything she knew about the mystery renter.

He already claimed the top three attributes in the small-town matchmaker's handbook. Single. Tall. And, most importantly, employed. But also *apparently* he was handsome in a *rough around the edges* way, Mrs. Waverly had whispered. "He just needs a woman's touch, I think."

Kaitlin had stifled a smile when her seventy-eight-year-old landlady had then winked.

Because Kaitlin was single, could cook and didn't have a parade of men in and out of her home—what Mrs. Waverly disdainfully referred to as *dating around*—she had also passed muster with her matchmaker landlady. In fact, it seemed she was a special case. The double-edged sword of being a virgin with a reputation for not putting out was guaranteed to keep most men at arm's length, or rather, far, far away. At least it had been in her disappointed experience.

She hadn't started out that way. She'd gone out with a few men over the years. Men she'd thought were interested in more than just trying to get her between the sheets to add a notch to their bedposts. But then the inevitable day came when these men expected her to spread her legs and let them do whatever they wanted so they could move on to the next girl. Kaitlin, at the time, felt like she deserved more. She certainly wanted what she considered the gift of her virginity to go to someone who'd appreciate it.

Then she wised up to reality. That dream died a painful death. But if she was going to give it up to someone, Kaitlin wanted it to be a prime male specimen and not just a love 'em and leave 'em bedpost-notch seeker.

She'd had bad luck in the "finding a decent male" department. Instead of decent, the only men she'd discovered were pricks. Did she have a prick magnet embedded somewhere perhaps?

All she'd wanted was someone who was interested and wanted to be with only *her*, to talk to her, laugh with her, look forward to seeing her. Not to chase her relentlessly until she gave in, regardless of any other trait she carried. Unfortunately, the latter had been her typical dating experience.

No more. She had a new plan. If only Zak would cooperate.

Still seated on his motorcycle, Zak revved the engine. Her heartbeat sped up. Zak always did that right before he turned the engine off, stood, twisted at the waist and dismounted. Woo boy. That was the premium move she waited to see each and every day.

What a gorgeous tenant the new bad-boy renter had turned out to be. He was as attractive as he was completely wrong for her, making him all the more desirable. That, coupled with the motorcycle he rode every day, made him a dangerous temptation. A tall, muscular, employed and attractive inducement.

Her eyes slid shut in contemplation of being embraced in his strong arms, and what it would feel like when they kissed for the first time. What it would feel like if they came together erotically as men and women did. She wanted to know what it felt like *to come together erotically* with a man at long last.

She fantasized that one day he'd take her for a ride, and not only on his motorcycle. A rush of heat filled her from face to toes, along with the sudden vision of a naked, sweaty Zak moving above her, his copious muscles bunching and relaxing as they made love. What would his slick, hard body feel like pressed deliciously against hers? Or pressed *inside* her? Having never been naked against any man, she could only imagine.

In her fantasy, he would be perfect. Secretly a gentleman willing to wait until they tied the knot for sex, if she wanted it that way. Whether or not they made their relationship sexual, he'd love her unconditionally. He'd think she was smart, capable and worthy. He'd never call her names. He'd never make her feel bad about herself. He'd always champion her.

No doubt Kaitlin would be disappointed if she ever got up the nerve to speak to him, but the fantasy lived on. Well, at least it had until she'd gotten that call from her stepsister this morning. Then the timetable had shifted dramatically.

Kaitlin had waited for him each and every day since he'd moved in a few weeks ago, longing for the courage to speak to him in person, initiate a conversation, and to ask him if he might be interested in helping her with her plan. The "I don't want to be a virgin any longer" plan. The private plot that needed to be taken care of sooner rather than later.

Beyond the fact that she thought Zak very attractive, she suspected he wasn't the type of man who'd want to settle down and get married—the biggest stereotype of all for a bad boy, and that was exactly what she needed.

Kaitlin had been on the hunt for a man to provide one very important service. But she needed the relationship to be temporary. And what would *he* get out of it? Sex. But was sex with a complete novice enough? It would have to be. That was all she had to offer.

Meanwhile, she'd lose her virginity once and for all to someone she didn't know. Someone she wouldn't have to see all the time. *Unless she looked out her window.*

Someone who wouldn't seek her out each and every day in this small town, knowing what she looked like naked. Someone who would be unlikely to whisper behind her back to her friends and acquaintances that she was inadequate and old-fashioned because she wouldn't put out on a first date.

It wasn't like she and Zak travelled in the same circles. She'd never seen him at the library, the local park, or even the grocery store in the few weeks he'd lived here. And she'd looked. The only time she saw Zak was when she pulled the living room curtain aside and watched with prurient fascination from just feet away as he dismounted his motorcycle. He was damn near perfect.

A humiliating memory slid into her mind, a reminder of the town she'd grown up in after age nine. A town she'd left the summer after graduating from college thanks to the vicious gossip of those who'd attained the status of Somebodies who looked down on folks just trying to get by. Kaitlin's reputation for being a virginal tease, an unfair label that her stepsister, Brooke Bailey, perpetuated with each visit, had followed her to her new home. At least she wasn't going to be here forever.

Kaitlin pushed her stepsister and her antics to the back recesses of her mind as she watched Zak on his motorcycle. Anticipation built in her core, among other tingly places.

There were three reasons she hadn't already chosen a random guy in this town for an initial hookup. First, she knew too many people. Second, no one had ever been remotely interesting. Lastly, she'd given up on ever settling down here and having a family.

She fully expected that when she finished her contract with her employer, she'd move on to bigger and better things out of this small town. But that was at least a year away. And besides she was lonely.

The loud throttle of his engine rattled the glass panes in every one of her windows. With a final loud engine rev, Zak turned the motor off and put the kickstand down.

He sat there, pulled his helmet from his head, shook his mane of curly dark locks like some rock star coming off stage after a concert, and *then* slowly stood. He swung one long muscular leg over the seat, easing off the black leather with the smooth grace born of those in truly great shape.

Watching Zak dismount from his motorcycle made the space between her thighs weak, moist and needy. Just as seeing him for that very first time had done.

If this wicked feeling was what put people together in sweaty, sexy compromising positions, Kaitlin wanted to try it. This bad boy was the first to ever elicit such a core-tightening response in her.

He leaned over and hung his helmet on one handle, which tightened the fabric of his blue jeans gloriously over his well-shaped butt.

His ass was a work of art.

Kaitlin was unprepared when he suddenly turned his head and stared in her direction. Heart in her throat, she dropped the curtain, stepped away from the window and pressed herself to the wall, trying to hide.

It was truly a ridiculous move.

How was she supposed to seduce him if she couldn't even get up enough nerve to stare back when he looked her way? She was pitiful, when the opposite was called for. She needed to do something bold. A streak of bravery stiffening her spine, she stepped back to the window and yanked the curtain aside. Disappointment filled her. He'd already moved to his porch. He likely also thought she was a pathetic fool.

Maybe tomorrow when he rode up on his loud motorcycle, she could make a plate of freshly baked muffins, knock on his door, and then talk him into bed once his mouth was full of sweet, fruit-filled confection. She glanced at the kitchen counter where the blueberry muffins she'd pulled out of the oven cooled in the muffin tins.

No. That wouldn't work.

Brooke would be here early in the afternoon. Snotty. Superior. Smug. Ready to share her latest sexcapades.

Kaitlin needed to do something today. She glanced at the muffins again as a new plan circulated in her brain.

Time was wasting.

She needed to do something bold and she needed to do it right now.

Brooke would be here tomorrow in full brag mode and ready to belittle Kaitlin and her non-existent sex life. That thought alone spurred her to find any shred of her courage.

Today, Kaitlin had additional incentive to ignore her shy nature and ask Zak an important question. "Will you have sex with me right now?"

Brooke, Kaitlin's older, worldlier stepsister, was coming for a visit. Kaitlin didn't want her to come, but somehow she always lacked the grit to keep Brooke from doing whatever the hell she wanted to do.

If Brooke wanted to damn well visit, nothing on God's green earth would stop her, certainly not Kaitlin's protests or fabricated excuses. So she sucked up her anger and packed it away in the crowded area of her mind reserved especially for her difficult stepsister.

Brooke had been an outrageously spiky thorn in Kaitlin's side since the day they'd met. Their parents had married in a quiet ceremony before Kaitlin and her two brothers had a chance to meet their new stepsister. Kaitlin might have told her mother not to do it if she'd discovered Brooke's true personality before the nuptials.

There were several topics of difficult conversation Brooke could instigate once she arrived for her visit, all designed to make Kaitlin painfully aware of everything Brooke had that she didn't. Kaitlin should number them for simplicity.

One, she'd brag about her latest wealth-bringing job that Daddy had helped her get.

Two, perhaps she wanted to name drop the most recent star she'd been hanging out with, wasting time and money on superficial pursuits. She hadn't droned on about those things in a long while.

Number three was a recurring favorite of Brooke's: her latest sexual conquest of the best-looking, richest man sporting the biggest dick *ever* in recorded history. Brooke Bailey, more tolerated enemy than friend or stepsister, loved nothing better than to regale Kaitlin with stories of her scandalous sex life. Brooke knew Kaitlin was a virgin and seemed to take personal joy in the fact.

Topic number three was almost always the reason she visited so often.

Brooke was mean and cruel about the details, too. She'd begin telling Kaitlin about some tantric sex position with a man sporting a ten-inch cock, then stop, laugh and say something along the lines of, "Oh, but you don't even know what I'm talking about. You're still a *virgin*," as though virginity was a disease to be ashamed of.

Just once Kaitlin wanted the conversation not to circle around to her limited personal knowledge of sex.

Hence her plan for Zak to relieve her of her hated innocence.

One time, just one single time, Kaitlin would like to be one up on Brooke. Just once she wanted to act nonchalant about a recent affair and teasingly withhold the details because she actually *had* a sex life instead of not having anything at all to share.

She'd even tried lying during Brooke's last visit, insisting she wasn't a virgin anymore. Not only did Brooke threaten to tattletale to their parents, she then asked pointed questions, doing her best to catch Kaitlin in the lie. Kaitlin didn't have answers because she didn't actually know firsthand, for example, what a man's dick looked like fully erect. Not beyond what she'd learned in sex ed, that is. And she'd been too ashamed to look up pictures online or in a book in the library. What if someone caught her?

Nor did she have the first clue what it felt like to have that fully erect dick buried to the hilt in her body. Sure, she'd read about it, but her paltry imagination was no match for Brooke, the ultimate sexpert. Kaitlin couldn't pull off the bluff.

When Brooke had called her on it, Kaitlin had told her weakly that she'd only been kidding and faked a laugh.

Thrilled, Brooke became even more obnoxious. She'd gone on and on about poor, pitiful Kaitlin having to invent a relationship because she didn't have what it took to attract a real man to fuck her. It had been horrible.

Kaitlin knew she shouldn't care what Brooke thought, but after half a lifetime of her stepsister's ridicule, she just wanted to win once. She deserved a big check in the winner's column one effing time, didn't she?

The moment she heard Brooke's throaty voice over the phone this morning, Kaitlin immediately thought about her continued virginal status and how she didn't want it any longer. Her next thought had been about her bad-boy neighbor, more specifically, his perfect ass.

Truthfully, she'd been looking for candidates to remove her virginity since she'd moved to town. Her selection was limited to strangers passing through or temporary residents planning to move on soon, but she hadn't found any.

Until Zak moved in.

Contrary to Mrs. Waverly's assumptions, Kaitlin didn't think he was planning to stay in this small town for the six months of his lease. From the little she had observed, he seemed like someone who moved around a lot, making him the perfect man for her needs. It was another stereotype, but she hoped it was true.

After she'd started watching Zak on a regular basis, Kaitlin wanted to know more than ever what it felt like to have sex, and her interest had nothing to do with Brooke and her foolish cruel streak. Even if Zak stayed in town longer than six months, she still wanted to learn the secrets of passion, skin-to-skin contact, sex, and most of all kissing. From him.

She'd been kissed before. However, not one kiss had been the stuff sonnets were written about. Maybe it was her. Perhaps she didn't inspire the kind of kiss she dreamed about. The usual dry, quick contact—feeling much like a hen pecking up corn from a barnyard—hadn't inspired her to want more.

She wanted a real kiss. A lip-licking, tonsil-tickling French kiss that she'd hold dear for a lifetime and fondly remember on her deathbed. Was that so much to ask?

Not only did Zak have a wickedly sensual mouth, but just watching him straddle his motorcycle made all manner of things in her body tingle and moisten every time she saw him. He made her pulse spike and her heart thud hard enough to break through her chest. Kaitlin needed to ask him if he'd be interested in having sex with her. Soon. Now.

Starting a conversation with Zak would be difficult, since she could barely stare at him without breaking out in heat. That was irrelevant. Do or die, any sex would have to take place this afternoon or tonight. Brooke would be here tomorrow.

CHAPTER TWO

Zak watched the recently vacated window, smiling as he saw the curtains flutter. His prim, sexy neighbor was staring at him again. Given the many women showing up at the garage to stare, drool or attempt to lure him away, he figured she was another in a long line looking for a bad boy to satisfy whatever fantasies good girls conjured up.

He was flattered, of course, at all the attention. It didn't hurt his ego a bit to have women chasing after him on a daily basis. But none of them were as intriguing or as enticing as his reclusive next-door neighbor.

Zak had taken note of her as soon as he'd moved in. The only time she came outside was to feed the homeless cat who'd taken up residence on her back porch. The first time she bent over to put a bowl of food down for the little beastie, ninety-nine percent of his blood flow had gone south, leaving him light-headed but smiling. The view of her ass was quite spectacular. In fact, the rest of her was also very easy on the eyes and a pleasure to watch.

He knew from his landlady that her name was Kaitlin and she worked as a bookkeeper for the school district.

She was pretty. Obviously shy. He'd be lying if he said
he wasn't more than a little intrigued. But he wasn't
chasing after her. It wasn't why he was here. He had
something to take care of, hopefully in the short term,
and then he'd be gone to the next undercover job.

Although, of all the women seeking him out, she was
the only one he'd be hard-pressed to ignore. If she got up
enough courage to approach him, he'd at least chat with
her. It would be the neighborly thing to do.

They hadn't been *officially* introduced, but his
landlady had been quick to tell him there was a very nice
single girl living next door. He knew Mrs. Waverly,
bless her heart, wanted to match them up in the worst
way, but that wasn't a good idea for a whole host of
reasons.

The first, and most important, was he didn't plan on
being here much longer. It would be wrong to start a
relationship with a nice single girl from this small town,
and then ditch her without a word when his job was
done.

Secondly, his demanding, dangerous career didn't
lend itself well to girlfriends, especially sweet ones like
he suspected his neighbor was.

And finally, Zak Thornton wasn't his real name. It
was a total dick move to romance a girl using a fake
name and a fake life. Knowing the fluid way this job was
going, he could be here one hour and gone the next. It all
depended on the lowlife scumbags he was hanging out
with and their criminal plans.

Honestly, he hadn't expected to attract any attention.
In his mind, he looked like a ragged beast. Perhaps the
bad-boy persona he'd copied for this job had unintended
consequences. Like attracting a nice girl looking to
reform a bad boy. Next time he'd think his look through
better.

There were some pluses to his Thornton alias. He

didn't have to shave regularly or keep his hair cut to a military length, and he got to ride a badass motorcycle. But it was all a facade. His rugged look, shaggy-haired and unshaven, suited the man he was supposed to be. While Zak Thornton was exactly the kind of man who would love to hook up with the nice single girl next door for a quick, satisfying fuck as needed, Zak Langston wasn't the kind of guy who'd use a woman for his own convenience.

Especially not one he'd never see again.

Undercover for over three weeks, not counting the week of prep before he arrived here, his connections had brought him to this small town and the bad guy flavor of the month he was after. He'd carefully crafted this persona to match what Diego Demarco would expect. But even with the best grungy bachelor perks, Zak was ready for this assignment to be over. He wanted to get back to his regularly scheduled life. Such as it was. And often, it was lonely. Until the next job from The Organization came along to occupy his time.

How much longer did he plan to do this shit? He didn't know. He longed for the day when the nice girl next door would be one he could actually take the time to pursue. As much as he looked like a badass fucker of nice girl-virginal types, chasing after his own pleasures at all times regardless of the consequences, he wasn't that man.

Zak glanced up at the window again. He didn't see her. She usually didn't take a second peek after he looked over, but most days he wished she would. Perhaps she only noted his arrival on the loud motorcycle. The ride he wished he could keep after this mission. His bike was sweet. Would the girl next door maybe want a ride on it? Or maybe a ride on him?

The sudden vision of his prim and proper neighbor hugged up behind him on the leather seat, her arms clenching his middle as he wove through cones laying the bike down on one side then the other as he tried to scare her into hugging him tighter, filled his imagination and also stirred his dick in a more amorous direction.

The curtains at the window were still moving a bit.

Maybe one of these days he'd surprise her and knock on her door. He wondered what she'd say, what she'd do. Would she invite him in? Make him dinner? Take him to bed?

Reality stepped in and slapped him on the back of the head. He'd secured this rental for six months, but knew now it wouldn't take that long to complete this mission. The job he was on would likely be over in a matter of a week or two, probably less. He didn't need to start anything with his nice neighbor, no matter how attractive she was.

Luckily, she seemed too shy to initiate anything herself. As long as he kept his distance, he'd be fine. And very soon he'd be gone. She'd be a memory he'd treasure. Perhaps he'd come back as his real self and see if she recognized him all cleaned up, shaved, shorter hair and driving his four-door sedan.

But would she even be interested in his real, non-bad-boy self?

He shook his head. That was a bad idea.

Zak forced his mind back to the job at hand. He was waiting for a phone call that the *deal* he'd proposed would be accepted. Once they made the trade, his cash for the illegal merchandise promised, Zak would go on his merry way. As soon as the local gang spent even one dollar of the money, the feds would be all over them.

Sometimes Zak stuck around to be arrested, too, but this was a different setup. He didn't have to be arrested to maintain his cover. He was only here to initiate the ultimate takedown and let the criminals hang themselves by spending dirty money and spreading it around to all their associates. This might be a digital age, but cash was anonymous and still ruled many illegal operations.

Zak walked to the front of his rented house. He actually looked forward to coming home at night. Furnished housing was always preferable, and Mrs. Waverly had done a nice job with this place. He'd make sure and check in the after-report for any repercussions against this rental. He'd make an anonymous donation to his also very nice landlady in case there were reprisals after he was gone. Once Demarco learned that the money was tainted, he might send thugs here to trash the place. It wasn't uncommon. It had certainly happened before.

The ancient land-line phone rang in the house as he entered. His first thought was that his shy neighbor was finally calling him. Maybe Mrs. Waverly had given her his number. He picked up before the end of the third ring.

"Yes," he said into the receiver with a much softer tone than he usually reserved for the scumbag criminals he associated with.

"You need to get down here. Something's up." Julio sounded panicked. The guy who'd helped him get a meeting with the local target dealer was usually pretty calm.

It was Julio's own fault he was in the position he found himself in. Still, when all was said and done, Zak hoped to get him out of it if he cooperated with The Organization.

It wasn't a coincidence they worked at the same garage. Julio had been Zak's initial target as a possible way into the tightly-knit organization Zak's superiors wanted taken down. His father had founded the group, and Julio was a reluctant member.

Julio might have to spend the rest of his life in

witness protection, but only if all went well here. Zak hoped Julio would be smart enough to take whatever the federal system offered him to start a new life, but he couldn't force him.

"What's wrong?" Zak asked, keeping his voice deliberately calm.

"Diego is on his way to the Playground." The bar on the outskirts of town, aptly called the Devil's Playground, was Demarco's unofficial headquarters and where he did the bulk of his eclectic business.

"Right now? I thought he was out of the country until next week."

"One of his lieutenants just got picked up on a weapons charge. He's in jail out in LA pending arraignment. Diego is worried someone set his guy up."

"He won't talk, will he? The lieutenant?" Zak silently rooted for Diego's LT to do just that. Spill his guts, tell every little detail, and make Zak's job here easier.

Julio made a snorting noise. "Nah. He'll do a full prison stretch before giving up a hint of information."

"So why is Diego worried?" Zak pushed out a silent breath and hoped this complication didn't impact his work here.

"Diego's afraid there's a rat in his organization. Now he's being cautious of all new associations."

Fuck. This was not going to help Zak with his undercover operation. In fact, it was the opposite of help. Unfortunate, since he'd already invested quite a bit of time, manpower and a healthy amount of his division's financial resources into it, including the six-month rental agreement for a great price on a nice rental house owned by an even nicer landlady.

"He's changing things up to flush out the traitor. He's trying not to be predictable, you know?"

"Yeah. Sure. Understandable, I guess. Whatever." Zak pretended indifference when inside his gut churned as he speculated on the fallout of pulling up stakes here and canceling this job.

"How fast can you get here? Diego's ready to meet with you to discuss the deal today."

"I thought he was being cautious."

"He is. But the sooner you can convince him you're legit, the sooner he can move on to someone else, you dig?"

"Right." *Fuck.*

"Are you on the way here, man? You should already be on your bike. I don't hear it."

"Getting there quickly is not the problem, Julio." He moved toward his front door. "Doing the deal today instead of next week is obviously much sooner than I expected."

"Are you in or not?"

"I'm in," he said quickly. "I'll be out there to deal, but I won't have the cash on me, right? I don't just have my cash sitting around in my place, you know what I mean? Any problem with that?"

Julio was quiet for the space of three heartbeats. "I'm vouching for you, Zak. You better not double-cross Diego and come up empty handed, or he'll take it out on both of us."

Zak well knew Demarco's view on those who disappointed him. Typically, he eliminated them quietly, and well before any other justice could be served.

"Julio, come on. It's me. Why would I do that? I have the payroll to purchase his product and a very lucrative new market to sell it in. I came into some cash from a benefactor and now both of us will get rich. Besides, this isn't the only deal I intend to do. This is just a first-time buy to get the introductions out of the way. The thing is, it would be stupid to keep that kind of cash here with me, right?"

"I guess—"

Zak cut him off. "Do you carry that kind of cheddar, Julio?"

"No." The tone of his voice said he finally understood Zak's dilemma. "You're right, Zak. You'd be stupid to in this town."

"Exactly. I'm not stupid. So if the meet is right now, great. We'll meet and discuss the deal. But I won't have the money on me." *Because I also need time to have my tech guys put the trackers on the bills.* Technology these days fucking rocked. Like James Bond's best wet dream, there was little that wasn't possible in the world of gadgets.

"I can bring the bankroll back to him later in private after we hammer out the specifics of the arrangement." Actually, this would work out better. The payoff place didn't have to be in town. Maybe he could schedule it for miles out into the barren area between this town and the next. There would be less possibility of any civilian interference or casualties that way.

"Right. I hear you. Just be at the bar in ten minutes."

"Done. See you there."

Zak started to make a call on his cell phone to get his team working on the money, glancing at the wall clock as he moved to his front door. Demarco was also obsessive about meetings starting on time. Zak needed to leave in the next thirty seconds to make it to the bar in time.

Instead of a phone call, he sent a cryptic text to alert his handler and the higher ups that the deal was coming together sooner than expected. He grabbed his helmet and headed for the door he'd just come in. Later he'd make a call and have the tagged money delivered or put in a place he could direct Demarco and crew to.

He snatched the door open. His prim, sexy neighbor stood there, arm raised, obviously about to knock. She held a plate in one hand with a cloth napkin draped over the top. *Shit*. He didn't have time to deal with her. He barely had time to make it to the bar as it was.

Without acknowledging her verbally, he barged outside and turned his back on her as he locked the door behind him. Spinning around again, he saw her uncertain smile. Her mouth opened, and she said, "Hi. I wanted to offer a belated welcome—"

"Sorry. I'm in a hurry. I can't talk right now." The scent of warm blueberry muffins registered by the time he was halfway down his front stairs, jamming his helmet on his head. The other, more visceral, stimulating scent was all *her*. And he loved it. It was surely his imagination, but she smelled like sex. Unfortunately, now was not the time he could explore that.

Without looking directly at her, he got on his Harley, fired it up and quickly wheeled it around to do a wide U-turn in the shared driveway. A check in his mirror showed she was still on his porch when he roared away down the street, headed to what would hopefully be the end of his time here.

It was a shame they'd never connect.

It was just as well she'd waited too long to act. Zak would negotiate this deal, set up the place where the money could be stashed to pay for Demarco's premium merchandise and then disappear.

As soon as the cash was distributed and spent by the bad guys, the good guys would swarm in and arrest everyone. It was possible he'd be completely done with this job and this town before midnight tonight.

He admitted to himself it was very unfortunate that any attraction or future relationship with his shy neighbor would remain unexplored. Making her the only regret he had about leaving this place. The prim, sexy woman he'd just left standing on his rented porch with what smelled like home-baked blueberry muffins and a tantalizing female scent even now made his cock stiffen. The scene might always haunt him with sincere regret.

Fate was a cruel bitch, but his prim neighbor was better off without him complicating her life. No matter how much he wanted to explore her with leisurely care.

CHAPTER 3

Kaitlin watched Zak peel away on his bike. Anger stirred in her soul. Her heart was almost beating out of her chest in excitement. Her courage had finally shown up. She'd put on her sexiest dress and marched over to invite herself into his life, albeit briefly.

Her plan was to offer him homemade muffins, do her best to entice him, and finally to refuse to leave until he'd made her a woman by taking away her virginity as he satisfied his own salacious lusts with her innocent body.

When he'd breezed by her on the porch, the scent of leather and sexy male had assaulted her lungs. Her panties were saturated in a second. She almost dropped her plate to launch herself at him. Just as quickly, he'd shut his door, turned his back without so much as a by-your-leave and left her standing there like a fool with a plate of unwanted muffins.

Some seductress she turned out to be. Where was he headed in such an all-fired hurry? The motorcycle roared away like his ass was on fire. She'd seen him head west. There was only one place in that direction he could be going to before several miles of blacktop exited right out of town.

The Devil's Playground. A raunchy, rough bar on the wrong side of town.

How humiliating to be looked over and abandoned for such a place.

Anger bolstered her courage. She'd follow him. See if she didn't. If he kept rolling out of town, perhaps she'd stop in for a drink at the local biker watering hole and pick up someone *else* to take care of her escalating needs.

Before she could change her mind, Kaitlin marched back to her house to get ready to hunt him down. She pulled her hair out of the ponytail she usually wore, made use of her curling iron and applied plenty of hairspray to add volume to her stick-straight hair. An honest assessment of the dress she'd gone over to Zak's in yielded the honest personal opinion that she was still dressed too modestly.

Time to pull out the big guns.

The too low cut, way too tight knit dress Brooke had given her as a joke fit the bill perfectly. She retrieved the fuck-me black heels she'd bought on a whim last week. They went nicely with the clingy black-and-red knit dress she was almost wearing. She eyed herself critically in the mirror. The neckline barely held to the edges of her shoulders, revealing her bra straps like a middle-school kid playing dress up with Mommy's nice clothing.

The bra had to go.

Kaitlin pushed out a shaky breath. She hadn't gone out in public without a bra since she was fourteen. Tossing her best Victoria's Secret in the laundry hamper, she slid the dress back into place. The soft fabric slipped like a whisper across her bare breasts. She studied herself in the mirror again as her heart pounded.

It looked pretty good. She still needed more, though.

Instead of the usual swipe of mascara and faint pink

lip-gloss she used day-to-day, she applied a thick black smear of eyeliner along each set of her lashes. Three coats of mascara and the painful process of curling them with a small torture device, and she suddenly had big eyes like the ones in magazines. *Perfect*.

A quick survey in the mirror of herself in the sexy dress and glam makeup showed a woman she almost didn't recognize. She was motivated to change, and her time had run out. Kaitlin needed to get rid of her virginity tonight. Her stepsister would be here tomorrow. If she was determined to do this, now was the time. If she couldn't entice someone wearing this dress, it was hopeless anyway.

She put a long black jacket over her sexy outfit for the sake of immediate modesty and headed out to her car. It was entirely possible that Zak had gone somewhere else after leaving, but she'd seen his bike parked at the Devil's Playground once before. Her anger had cooled enough for her to revise her goal. If she didn't see Zak there, she'd abandon her plan to fuck anyone else. Honestly, she didn't really want to have sex with any other stranger.

Kaitlin, to her relief, spied Zak's large black motorcycle before she even pulled into the gravel parking lot. Leaving her purse in the trunk, she put her keys, ID and some cash in her jacket pocket and took a deep breath. She could already hear the music, so it must be loud inside the bar.

She walked to the door, pulled it open and stepped into darkness. The neon sign behind the bar was seemingly the only light in the place. The dim, windowless space with a scattering of tables smelled like beer, sweat and all the things her mother had warned her to avoid in life. She held tight to her recently captured courage and pressed forward, gaze searching for Zak. He wasn't readily apparent. Was he in the back?

Five steps into the place, she felt a hand grip her ass and squeeze. She jumped forward as a voice said, "Hey, mama. Never seen you in here before. You looking for a date?" She turned to see the seated man who'd grabbed her put his hand between his legs and cup his package. "I'm ready to help you out, mama. I'll make you purr like a kitten."

Kaitlin decided then and there she wasn't capable of pulling this off. What a fool she'd been. If she got out of here without being violated, murdered and her body buried out back, she'd count herself lucky and never, ever take such a foolish risk again.

She took a step backwards, inching her hands behind her as if she could summon the door by reaching for it with her fingertips. Unfortunately, someone had moved in behind her, blocking her from the front door exit. She tucked her hands to the front to keep from accidentally touching the new stranger barring her escape.

"Don't go," the new scary stranger said. "You don't have to leave, sweetness. Stay. Have a drink. Relax." He smelled like booze, cigarette smoke and body odor. Kaitlin swayed forward to escape the stench of the man crowding her.

"I...I've made a mistake," she said in a barely audible voice. She clutched her hands to her coat collar, wishing she didn't look like a total slut beneath the thin covering.

The man behind her moved a step closer. He reached for her neck. She flinched but couldn't move fast enough before he grabbed her coat half off of her shoulders.

Arms trapped, Kaitlin went cold with panic. She froze as he tugged, trying to get her coat off.

"Loosen up. Let me take your coat," he said. A quick decision made her relinquish the coat. She wanted free of him. Losing the coat meant she was able to move away from him, albeit without her covering. With her long coat clutched in his fingers, his gaze went straight to her chest, dipping down to her unbound breasts.

Kaitlin took a longer step away from him and eyed the coat longingly. Her wallet and keys were in the pocket. But he still stared at her chest. She turned away. He laughed. Over her shoulder she saw him turn to hang it on a coat rack by the front door.

Decent of him, and a surprise.

She took a step or two further into the bar area, not looking exactly where she was going. Keeping her coat in view seemed more important in that moment. Then again, walking blindly further into this bar might also be unwise. So she divided her attention between scanning the bar for Zak and keeping an eye on her coat. With her head turning every which way, she was fairly certain she looked idiotic.

There were a few tables strewn about in her immediate surroundings. An arched open doorway ten feet ahead of her led into a larger room. Along the right side was a long wooden bar, where men sporting leather and denim and stitching that she assumed denoted various group affiliations sat on barstools.

Unfortunately, moving away from the man who took her coat also pushed her deeper into the bar, closer to the loud music, and further from the only way she knew out of this possibly dangerous place. Her gaze darted here and there throughout the dark space.

Still no Zak in sight.

Her attention was directed over one shoulder, focused on the man who'd taken her coat. He was again encroaching on her space. She moved almost sideways to keep the distance between them. A grin shaped his cruel lips. The jagged pink scar across his forehead didn't make him look dashing. It made him look scary. The stringy dark hair hanging to his narrow shoulders also didn't add any appeal.

What had she been thinking even coming inside this place? Why was she even here? Her stupid pride. Her stupid, foolish, longstanding need to one-up her worldly, older stepsister, that's why.

Brooke was the one person who'd *never* be impressed by Kaitlin's actions anyway. She was about to die thanks to making poor decisions regarding her foolish lack of experience with men. Maybe she deserved to be buried out back.

She'd push out a dejected sigh, but didn't want to draw any more attention to herself than she already had by bursting in here like an idiot junior high girl chasing after the unattainable bad boy.

Kaitlin swore that if she got out of this mess she'd never want or try to get sex ever again. Brooke could do her worst. And she would. Kaitlin vowed to suffer her many regrets in silence.

She'd let Brooke—

Her self-flagellating reverie was interrupted when the man who'd grabbed her ass and spoken initially—a slightly rotund older man with a fading hairline—suddenly stood up and moved in her direction.

Kaitlin took two quick steps further into the bar to avoid being sandwiched between him and the coat thief. She made it to the arched doorway and rushed into the next room, her shoulder leading the way, without much thought as to where she was headed.

Three steps past the entryway, her attention still wasn't on where she was going. Naturally, she bumped into someone. Out of the corner of her eye she saw dark hair, smelled expensive cologne, and felt the power of the man's presence when he moved a single stride closer.

She looked up into the face of another scary man. He was devastatingly handsome in a completely demonic sort of way. He sported a large smile filled with straight white teeth and an angular, sculpted face any male model would kill for, but his eyes were dark and dead. The large grin shaping his lips never came close to reaching his gaze with any form of real amusement. Like a grinning shark.

His deep voice grated across her skin unpleasantly when he said, "What do we have here? A new customer?" His gaze dropped to Kaitlin's braless, low-cut cleavage. She wanted to cover herself with her hands, but feared looking even more ridiculous.

Everyone in the immediate area looked at the man with respect. Or maybe it was fear. Either way it was clear this satanically attractive and powerful man was the boss.

She was so screwed. Her boobs fairly hanging out of the slutty dress she wore, Kaitlin was also without the means to leave. She'd lost sight of her coat, but hoped it was still by the front door, even though she wasn't.

Now the powerful man likely in charge of this heathen space was about to make a decision that would probably change her life forevermore. Would he accost her? Put her into a white slavery ring where her virginity would be auctioned off to the highest bidder? *I do have a fanciful imagination along with my potent death wish, trying to get laid for the first time in a biker bar no less.*

Kaitlin's eyes filled with frightened tears. It was a huge tactical mistake to show fear in a place like this and in front of a man like this. Knowing that didn't stop the growing panic infusing her soul with dire predictions of what was about to happen. Terror soaked into the very marrow of her bones. She was going to die because she'd futilely lusted after a man and sought out the pleasures of the flesh.

She took a step away from the boss, bumped into the rotund man crowding her. She side-stepped him and turned, ready to run toward a hallway she hoped would lead her to the back exit, only to plaster herself against the muscular front of the man she'd come in here to find.

Zak.

The masculine scent of him hit her first, infusing her lungs with pleasure, arousal and, most importantly right now, a sense of refuge. Pressed this close to him, Kaitlin felt immediate comfort, inherent desire, and debilitating lust with every breath she took. Without another thought, she wrapped her arms around his waist, locking her hands at the small of his back, hugging him tight, and pressing her breasts to his solid abs.

She wasn't going to let go. They'd have to pry her off.

"What are you doing here, Kaitlin?" Zak's low voice rolled over her. *He knows my name?*

She tilted her head back when his irate tone registered. It didn't support any notion of safety. Her gaze locked with his deep blue eyes.

"Zak," she said with the appropriate amount of fear laced into the word, wanting to cry because she had assumed she would be safe in his arms. Currently she was unsure he'd be any better than anyone else here. All she really knew about him was that he had a great ass and Mrs. Waverly liked him.

An unruly lock of his hair dropped to the center of his forehead. Despite her terror, she wanted to tuck it back in place. She wanted to lovingly stroke his whiskered face. She wanted to trace the beautiful lines of his sculpted lips with a light touch before discovering what he tasted like.

Her heart sped in her chest as several intimate desires filled her body and soul. "I didn't like how we left things on your front porch," she finally said. She'd thought her words were stated quietly enough that only Zak could hear it.

But behind her, Mr. Demonic Power asked, "Fighting with your woman, Zak?" He made a *tsk tsk* noise.

Zak's gaze lifted to the boss man.

"No," he said, crushing her feelings. She wasn't his woman, unfortunately. They'd never formally met or even touched until now. Why did she expect he'd save her?

"No? Are you sure? Sounds like you left your woman behind and now she's caught up with you."

"Well, some jackass called and told me I needed to get here right now or else. Did you think I was just sitting by the phone waiting for your call?" Zak laughed. Kaitlin was close enough to feel the rumble of amusement fill his wide chest. But he didn't sound happy at all. "Well, I wasn't just sitting around doing nothing, was I, baby?"

Both of Zak's arms wound around her with measured care. His palm pressed warmly in the center of her back, pushing her more intimately into his firm body. Her hips settled against his erotically, one pelvic bone digging in, invading her side. *Baby? Was he going to play along and save her? Please?*

Was it wrong to like the way he called her *baby*, like intimacy had already been shared between them? Like they were already rolling around in his bed, beneath the sheets, taking every opportunity to go at it like bunnies as often as possible?

A warm, loose feeling encompassed her as that fantasy swirled in her head.

"No. You weren't just sitting around," she murmured near his collar. "You were about to be very busy...with me." *Because I was about to seduce you, but you had to leave and come here to see the beautiful demon boss of this scary place. Now I understand. Now I wish I'd waited at home for you to return.*

Without warning, Zak's fingers brushed along her jawline, slipping easily into the waves of hair at the side of her face. The tips of his nails grazed a path along her scalp with a delicious, decidedly powerful force until his fingers curled through several locks and gripped tight.

He tugged her head back slowly until her face tilted upward. Her gaze was suddenly fixed on the wickedly curved shape of Zak's mouth. It was a completely possessive move to make, and she really liked it. She willed him to kiss her, lifting her stare to his luscious bedroom-blue eyes.

And he did, shockingly enough.

His mouth lowered in the next second, pressed hard to hers. His warm, luscious tongue licked between her pliant lips, sending tendrils of pleasure through her body from head to toes. He overwhelmed her in every possible wonderful way.

Kaitlin moaned, curling her tongue around his, tasting him, devouring him, falling in love instantly with the commanding way he kissed her.

Even if she was murdered and buried out behind the bar today, she would at least die happy with the taste of Zak's exquisitely perfect kiss on her lips.

CHAPTER 4

The moan Zak heard soon after he initiated this kiss with his *not* so prim and proper neighbor resonated through to his very soul. *Jesus*. This was so *not* the situation he wanted to instigate a lip lock with Kaitlin. He would have preferred to go back in time, pull her from his front porch and spend his time with her tucked away in the upstairs bedroom he'd claimed.

He would have rather pushed her to the surface of the soft bed and discovered why she seemed so fascinated with a bad boy instead of falling for a dentist or an accountant with a stable life, like she deserved.

Zak couldn't forsake her to this crowd. He'd have to claim her or Demarco would deal with her. A growing part of him didn't mind staking his claim so much.

After she moaned, he took inventory of all the places they were connected. First and foremost on his sizable list was the fact she'd ditched her bra and her soft ample breasts were pressed deliciously to his chest.

The notion equally tantalized and inspired dread because the crowd of onlookers was a dangerous one. He wasn't quite one of them yet. Once the first deal was completed, they'd feel he was complicit and trust him more, but not much. Bringing a woman into this place before the first deal was even arranged meant they would want to vet her as well. Now that he'd claimed her as his woman with such a provocative public kiss, his criminal life here was about to change.

They would all demand assurances that she wouldn't go around telling tales about their dealings—when, in fact, the business he'd rushed here to discuss hadn't even begun yet.

Tensions were already at deadly levels. Instead of getting down to business with Zak, Demarco had ranted and raved about his lieutenant being arrested. Everyone in the bar had listened with wide-eyed fascination like looky-loos passing a car wreck on the highway hoping to see blood, gore and mangled bodies.

Demarco's demeanor—showcasing angry eyes, verbose threats regarding all the nasty, bloodthirsty ways he'd get his revenge on those who'd wronged him, followed by completely manic and nearly out of control ranting—had subsided to shouting, but he still hadn't calmed enough to engage in a normal level of conversation.

Zak had seen him do the exact same thing the last time they'd met. Demarco had raged and threatened the world before calming to engage in steady conversation as if nothing was amiss, as if he'd only recently been discussing unpleasant weather.

Like last time, Zak determined to endure the crazy until Demarco wound down so they could get to the reason he was here.

Then the front door opened and Kaitlin walked in.

Some unseen signal apparently raced through the bar that a stranger had entered. Zak heard Julio curse under his breath and move away from him. Zak's heart had plummeted to his knees when he realized she must have followed him. He made a quick self-note: *Never leave a woman standing on a porch with blueberry muffins, no matter how deranged the criminal you're about to meet is.*

The heavy makeup and the huge change to her hairstyle and wardrobe were not lost upon him. She looked fucking hot. Likely he wasn't the only one here who thought so.

The lip lock had aroused him to a level that sent half the volume of his blood south of his belt buckle. His thickening response below wasn't made up, so he nudged her with it. He didn't want to scare her as much as try to keep them both alive in the next few moments.

She moaned again, tightening her grip around his waist. *Fuck.* Nope, she was not at all scared. But she should be.

"Get a fuckin' room, unless you plan to share her," said a voice from the growing crowd to his left. *Fuck that.*

He broke the fervent kiss, pulling away enough to stare down at her wet, swollen lips. He drilled a look in her eyes that warned her to keep quiet and let him handle this.

"Make no mistake. I *never* share," he said loudly over his shoulder in the general direction of whoever had thrown out the suggestion. Julio had disappeared. Probably not a good sign.

His gaze quickly turned to Demarco. "Give me two minutes to send my woman on her way, and we'll discuss what we need to." *Maybe you can also stop bitching about your lieutenant and we can get down to business.*

Demarco gifted him with that satanic grin again. "No need, my friend. She can stay."

Fuck that. If she stayed, she'd end up in witness protection, at best. Or at worst, a shallow grave near the bar. Either way, she wouldn't survive the day in her current lifestyle. Demarco had harsh rules for those who'd witnessed his business. They either became complicit in it or died.

Kaitlin's life was about to change drastically. *Fuck.*

A glance back down into her face was rewarding in an, *I've just satisfied my woman with a single kiss* way. But he needed her to cooperate. He needed her to remain silent as a church mouse and not listen in or be part of this coming deal. If she was fucked into an unconscious slumber, that might be an acceptable alternative. His dick thought the idea was downright brilliant.

"Zak?" she whispered. Absurdly, her frightened expression only heightened his lust. Her hips shifted. She brushed her pelvis erotically across the front of his jeans. His cock pulsed against her. Her eyes widened at the subtle movement. If they'd been alone he would have pushed her to the nearest flat surface, pulled up her dress and torn away any obstruction to entering her silken body in the most expedient way.

"Baby, I thought you understood that I'd be back later. You should have waited for me at home."

"I...I...I'm sorry. You're absolutely right." She swallowed hard. "I should have stayed at home and waited for you."

She released the grip she had around his waist, dropping her arms to her sides. Zak pulled his hand from her hair and placed it firmly on her shoulder. If he could get her out of here and safely on her way, it would be a miracle. She turned in his arms, her one hip pressing into his groin with arousing effect as she moved. If he made it out of here alive tonight, he'd head for her house and not just to ensure her safety. They needed to discuss whatever she'd been on his porch to talk about earlier. Obviously, he'd been mistaken about the extent of her interest.

Zak pressed one palm to her flat stomach. Her muscles tensed beneath his fingertips. The other hand he placed strategically at her breastbone, centered on her luscious, revealing cleavage. As he'd intended, Demarco's attention was momentarily drawn to her unbound breasts. *Let her go. Don't make me involve her in your dirty business, you fucking psycho bastard.*

"Jorge," Diego called to the bartender. "Get Zak's woman a shot of tequila. She looks thirsty."

"Yes, boss. Right away." Jorge made noises, getting the drink ready.

Fuck. That meant she was staying.

"I don't let my woman drink," Zak said somberly. Kaitlin stiffened in his arms the moment the word "let" crossed his lips.

As shy as she seemed to be, she certainly didn't like being told what to do. Inwardly he appreciated her spunk. Unfortunately, it wasn't going to help in this situation.

He pressed his palms harder into her front, allowing one hand to slip a ways, halfway covering one of her luscious breasts. The tip of his ring finger glanced across her nipple, which hardened at the merest bit of pressure.

Zak swallowed hard, cleared his throat, and put his focus back where it belonged—on his dangerous opponent, Diego Demarco.

He leaned down, chin grazing Kaitlin's shoulder. He kissed the space beneath her ear and barely whispered, "Get ready to move."

She stiffened again as he spoke, giving him a modicum of hope that when the time came she'd follow him to the back hallway, which led to the bathrooms and the only other exit.

Zak wanted to postpone this meeting, get her home, call his crew, and a whole bunch of other things that weren't going to happen.

To his right, a sudden movement sent his pulse to his

throat. It was just the bartender, with not one but two very generously filled shot glasses of tequila.

"Drink up," Demarco said. A predatory smile followed his invitation. "And if you don't let your woman drink, feel free to take both shots. My treat."

"Thanks," he said. *Fucking great.* Two shots masquerading as three when the situation was dangerous enough while stone-cold sober, let alone buzzed on cheap booze. *Sure, let me drink a lot now, too, so I'm even slower to react.*

Zak shifted Kaitlin, anchoring her to his side with one arm draped around her shoulders. He reached for the first shot and downed it in a single gulp. The fluid burned all the way to his acid-filled belly. He caught Kaitlin's stare as he grabbed the second shot glass. Instead of the anger he expected, she looked exceedingly grateful.

Her crushed feminist feelings at his high-handedness were at least one less issue to worry about. He'd take any win at this point.

Zak bolted down the second shot. It burned just as much as the first had, but the acid in his stomach had settled some with the realization Kaitlin wasn't mad at him. Foolish notion, but whatever.

He needed to get his woman out of here without causing chaos in this dangerous world or ending their lives. Being here in what sometimes seemed like an alternate universe often meant being continuously tested for loyalty. He couldn't say no to any generously offered food or drink. Ever. He couldn't let his woman show any public dominance or disrespect, especially not in Demarco's immediate surroundings.

Across the room, a lanky man, wearing a raggedy flannel shirt got down from a bar stool and approached the tense group. *Now what?*

"Kaitlin Price? What the hell are you doing here?"

Still attached to his side like they were a single entity, Kaitlin looked in the man's direction and sucked in a short, surprised breath. A frown followed her startled reaction.

Fuck. She obviously knew him.

This new twist did not bode well.

The man squinted and looked around at the assembled group, like he was surprised to find more people watching him than just Kaitlin.

His expression darkened. "You shouldn't be here, Kaitlin," he said. "Let me take you out of here to someplace quieter." He came closer, reaching one hand out as if he planned to remove her from the bar right now.

Mistake.

Kaitlin didn't move a muscle, but she subtly withdrew from his direction.

"Back off," Zak said in his most sinister tone. The guy didn't move. Zak wished getting her out of here could be as easy as having her walk out with this stranger. Even though he didn't feel comfortable with her in anyone's care but his own. Plus, Kaitlin didn't seem interested in leaving with him either. Now that Demarco was involved, he feared it was way too late anyway. No self-respecting thug would let his woman go off with another man under any circumstances.

Kaitlin pressed harder into the side of Zak's taller frame. "I'm fine right here."

Mr. Intruder suddenly frowned. The hostility in his expression was pegged at maximum and he inched even closer. Zak was going to have to punch the guy out. He was already an arm's length away.

Demarco, shockingly passive up to now, suddenly took an interest. "Why do you think she shouldn't be here, sir?"

The man swallowed hard and turned his attention to

Demarco, as if just realizing he shouldn't have interfered with such dangerous men. But then he shot a very unpleasant look at Zak. He backed up half a step.

"She's not the kind of girl who would be involved with a guy like him." *Dickhead.* "They can't be a couple."

Zak agreed with him, but couldn't show it.

Demarco turned a sharp gaze on Zak. "Is she truly your woman? I have to admit, I was surprised as well. You've never mentioned her. Not once. And with the stick-up-your-ass attitude, I would never have guessed you were getting laid regularly."

Zak narrowed his eyes. "She's mine. I came here for the deal you promised, not to shoot the shit about my sex life. If you don't want to make money, fine by me. You aren't the only one in this area with product to sell."

Keeping his arm firmly around Kaitlin, Zak took a step toward the front door, even though the back exit was closer.

"Not so fast." Demarco put a hand on his shoulder as if to hold him in place. He turned to the stranger who'd questioned Kaitlin's choice of boyfriend. "What makes you think they aren't a couple?"

His sullen gaze went to Kaitlin. "Everyone in town knows she's either frigid, a cocktease or both. She's never given any guy in town the time of day and now suddenly she's with *him*? I don't buy it."

Zak had only been here two weeks. In that time, he'd only seen her stare at *him*. He had no earthly idea about her history with men. He wouldn't even know what she did for a living except that his landlady had told him.

"If you expect me to push her to the ground and fuck her in front of a crowd to prove she's my woman, it's *not* going to happen!" His elevated voice at least made the man look nervous.

"No. Of course not." Demarco pointed a thumb over his shoulder. "You can use my private office."

Zak internally rolled his eyes. He'd been in Demarco's "private" office. It was an extra bathroom with a six-by-six-foot space attached. There was a sofa he wouldn't force a cockroach to touch and a small, beat-up desk with more splinters than wood holding it together. If they had sex in that room, he'd have to do her up against the safest, cleanest vertical surface, which was the flimsy door parading as privacy.

If they made any noise above a whisper, the entire bar would hear them even with the music turned up.

After that kiss, she could have no doubt he wanted her, but having their first time be in Demarco's dirty, skanky back office wasn't the romantic place she'd likely pictured. Then again, if it kept them alive and eventually got them out of here, it might be worth it.

The only other problematic question was whether there was a camera in there. Would he really have to do her up against the rickety office entry in case someone was watching or recording them for posterity, or simply make it *sound* good for those crowding around outside the door?

"Are you kidding me?" Kaitlin asked. "Who died and put you in charge of my love life, Arnold?"

Zak was surprised she spoke up at all. Her irate gaze settled on the man calling into question their previously non-existent relationship and her sensibilities regarding men. "In fact, it's none of your freaking business how we met. You're pissed off because I was never interested in giving *you* the time of day. Now you know why. I had *this* waiting for me at home." She glanced over one shoulder at Demarco and relaxed a bit against Zak. "However, in the interests of understanding our unusual connection, I'll explain. We met because he's my next-door neighbor. Does that make everyone happy now?"

Demarco's eyebrows rose. He settled his cool gaze back on Zak. "Is that so?"

"Yes," Zak said. He squeezed her tight. They were practically sealed together. "She knocked on my door with homemade blueberry muffins in hand to welcome me to the neighborhood, and the rest, as they say, is history." No one had to know their *history* had only started about an hour ago. A genuine smile graced Kaitlin's sultry lips as she stared up at him for a moment. Was she pleased he'd noticed what she'd brought him?

The man who'd accused her of being a frigid cocktease frowned, but didn't move away. Zak would make him answer for those unkind words later. For now, he wished he had the power to make "Arnold" disappear in a puff of smoke. Often, it sucked not having supernatural powers.

"I'd have to say it was love at first sight," Kaitlin murmured to Zak, but surely the others heard her.

Demarco lifted his arm and flicked his hand negligently at the man as if to swat away an annoying insect. Arnold didn't look happy, but luckily took the hint, melting away in the direction of his barstool without further comment or argument. A miracle.

Zak had a momentary glimmer of hope that he'd be able to get Kaitlin out of here alive without having to fuck her. Not that he didn't want her. In a perfect world, he wanted her to himself in a quiet cocoon of luxury.

The desire he felt for her was pretty much over the top after that amazing kiss. However, he didn't want to have sex with her in the bar's dirty back room. And most assuredly not for their first time together.

Given the choice, he wanted her in a bed far, far away from this place. Maybe in a tropical location, lingering inside a simple hut, on top of a soft bed with the beach on their doorstep and an ocean view, if they ever ventured from between the sun-dried sheets.

"Does this mean you're withdrawing the offer for us to use your private office?" Kaitlin asked. Zak almost uttered the words "what the fuck" out loud.

"No," Demarco said with an oily grin. "Please. Go right ahead."

Kaitlin made a small noise of protest when Zak promptly squeezed her hard enough to make his unhappy point regarding her scandalous request. Did she not understand what would happen in the back room?

"It's not necessary," Zak said in a low tone.

Demarco surveyed Kaitlin, then his prurient grin widened. "I believe it is. True love is at stake, my friend. Don't worry. Go take care of your woman. I'll wait until you're finished...satisfying whatever she wishes from you. I was the one responsible for callously calling you away from her unexpectedly. Please," he said, grinning like a demon, "take your time. I insist."

The most ruthless man in a hundred-mile radius walked toward the pool table they'd been about to use when Kaitlin had entered the bar. Zak didn't know if he was more alarmed by a suddenly tolerant Demarco willing to wait for him to *satisfy* his woman, or by the thought of how he'd accomplish whatever his "woman" wished from him without ending up starring in a lurid video sure to haunt him until his dying breath.

Strictly speaking, fucking a possible witness to a crime or, worse, an innocent bystander wasn't typically part of the code for allowable scenarios in The Organization's handbook.

However, if Demarco wanted him to have sex, he likely *did* have surveillance in the back office. The next question was whether it was video only or if anything they uttered in the heat of passionate advances would also be recorded.

Zak only had a few steps to explain far too much to his new woman.

He took a step toward the office door. "Are you out of your mind?" he asked softly, leaning close to her ear. Her delicious scent teased his senses. Not helpful. Not even close.

She gifted him with the most seductive, desire-filled expression he'd ever been impacted by in his life. "No. I just wanted..." she trailed off, staring into his eyes as if willing him to read her mind.

"You just wanted what?" *I yearn to do wild, wicked things to you, but not here, not in front of a possible audience, not in this bar's sleazy back room, not on video that might not only ruin my career if it's discovered, but your innocent privacy.*

"You," she whispered. "I wanted...you...needed you...in my bed...tonight."

CHAPTER 5

Kaitlin couldn't believe she'd gotten the words out that she wanted to say. She stared at him with all the hopeful intensity she could muster. He'd saved her. Walked right up, pretended to be her lover and saved her from the scary patrons in this darkly frightening environment. In her mind, heading for the back room to have sex was perfect. They'd both get what they wanted.

Zak looked so completely shocked she wanted to pull the words back from the air around them. Then again, what did she have to lose?

She wanted her virginity gone. It needed to happen tonight. The mere idea of Brooke's mocking laughter firmed her resolve.

He leaned close. "It's not that I'm unwilling to fuck you, baby, but the back room is not exactly the spot I would have chosen for our very first time. Not to mention it's probably bugged." His breath tickled the top of her ear.

"Bugged?" she asked when his words penetrated her haze of lust. She was already picturing what it would feel like to have sex for the first time. She couldn't wait. But did she want anyone watching her? As she considered the answer to that, Zak leaned in again.

"Demarco's got surveillance in there. He's known for his penchant for watching people have sex, taping it and selling the films. In fact, I hear it's his second favorite pastime." Likely she didn't want to know what Mr. Demarco's first favorite pastime was and had to bite her tongue to keep from asking.

The bar seemed to quiet, as if everyone in it was waiting to see them enter the back office space. She wondered if once the door was shut, every patron in the bar would hover right outside, a multitude of ears pressed to the painted surface, hoping to catch the sounds of the exuberant lovemaking they expected to hear.

She lost track of her thoughts when Zak wrapped his arms around her and kissed her mouth with the most seductive of intent. Then he whispered in her ear again. "We'll have to put on a good show, like we are really doing it. Are you up for that? If you're not, I need to know right now."

Kaitlin wrapped her arms around his neck. "I understand. I'm totally up for it." She pressed her mouth to his quickly, as if to seal their unholy alliance of lust. "In fact, we can *actually* do it if you want to."

"Sorry, baby. I didn't think to bring a condom with me."

"What? Why not?" Didn't men always carry them in a secret pocket of their wallets? Or was that merely another stereotype she'd always taken for the truth?

He laughed, and the sound seemed genuine. "Sex in this bar wasn't part of my original plans for this evening, baby." *Baby.* She enjoyed it very much when he called her that.

Upon quick consideration, the very idea of being watched or filmed having sex with Zak put her libido in the stratosphere. She didn't care that it wasn't what she pictured for her first time. She didn't care if she was filmed by some sex-crazed drug lord voyeur. If fact, she might ask for a copy to show Brooke when her stepsister refused to believe she wasn't a virgin any longer.

She wondered if she'd lost her mind.

"The thing is, we have to pretend we're already together. We have to make it look and sound like we've had sex before, lots. Follow my lead. I don't know if it's video only or if it will include sound. So don't forget that there's a camera or cameras somewhere in there."

Zak walked them over to a battered brown door that looked like it was a survivor of having more than one bottle of booze thrown against it in the heat of any number of bar brawls. He opened it and pushed her inside, followed quickly on her heels and closed the door behind them.

He walked past her and turned to lean his tight butt against the edge of the desk, putting several feet between them. He crossed his arms and frowned. "I'm not happy you followed me here, Kaitlin. I told you I had business."

Kaitlin looked around the room briefly, searching for where the camera might be but trying not to be obvious about it. The room had a single bare bulb hanging down from the ceiling. She couldn't imagine that any video would be of very good quality. This space was the definition of dingy. The smell of stale beer and pungent bleach likely masked even worse odors.

The only furniture was the battered old desk, with more gouges, scrapes and holes covering the top than available work surface, and a couch along one wall she mentally vowed not to touch for fear of an instant viral death. Not the ideal location for her first seduction. Plus, they had to act like they were *already* lovers. But she'd insisted they come back here, proving the level of crazy she'd reached in her zeal to one-up her stepsister.

Good or bad, whatever happened in the next few minutes was all on *her* head.

Her desperate need to get rid of her virginity as soon as possible had driven her to extreme lengths. She wasn't convinced that if she let Zak out of her sight he'd ever show up again. Either at his rental next door or his job at the garage, or anywhere else in town.

The moment the idea of the two of them retiring to the back room for satisfaction was on the table, she'd fought hard to make it happen. Standing in front of him now like an errant schoolgirl about to be disciplined for uncivilized actions, Kaitlin was starting to have second thoughts.

Perhaps she'd been a tad hasty. She didn't know Zak very well. Or at all. Just that he filled out his jeans nicely. Then again, he'd saved her from a very scary situation in the bar. He obviously had a good side. Perhaps this was an opportunity to ratchet the lust down a bit.

Maybe she could tell him to meet her later and then pray he'd show up to render his mighty cock repeatedly within her willing body to rid her of the virginity she'd grown to hate.

Remembering the role she had to play for the hidden camera, she said, "I'm sorry, Zak. I thought tonight was going to be just the two of us. I was really mad when you left me standing on your porch earlier."

"That has become very clear."

Kaitlin started toward him. He put his hand up. "Stop right there. The moment I smell you, my little head takes over. I'm not done talking yet."

"What else is there to discuss?"

"I know what everyone expects me to do in here, including you." He pushed out a sigh.

Kaitlin's breath caught. She whispered, "And will you do what everyone expects?" *Oh please. Oh please. Oh please.*

He stood and took two steps closer, towering over her, but not near enough to touch. "I shouldn't."

"Why not?"

"Because it rewards your inexcusably bad judgment. How can I ensure you won't do this again if I get a call and have to meet my friend, Diego Demarco, in the future?"

"I promise I'll never follow you again." He frowned, as though suspicious of her quick agreement. She stared up into his gloriously handsome face. "I promise, Zak." She held up two fingers in salute. "Scout's honor." She'd never been a Girl Scout, but she'd promise whatever it took to get him closer. Then maybe he'd "do" her.

"Scouts salute with three fingers." He took another step, settling his boot tips against her fuck-me black pumps. "And besides, promises are for little girls and virgins. And you are neither." *Hah*, she thought. *As far as you know.*

He must have read disagreement in her expression because his eyebrows went up meaningfully. Oh, right. They were playacting. Her brain disengaged every time he looked at her intensely. *But I* am *a virgin, until I talk you into bed. That's the problem.*

"Swear to me. Swear to me on your life that you'll *never* do this again."

"I swear it," she said with all the earnestness she could gather. "On my life."

His head dropped slightly. His luscious mouth swooped down to capture her lips in the most excruciatingly lust-driven kiss she had ever hoped to experience. He simply devoured her. She loved it.

The texture of his tongue swirling between her willing lips turned her on like she'd never, ever been tempted before. This was yet another kiss she'd remember on her deathbed, and also served to ratchet up her lust. He was very adept at making her want him. And she'd been at the level of slow simmer for a couple of weeks now.

Before she realized what was happening, her shoulder blades pushed against the flat surface of the flimsy door they'd come through. His hands roamed around her body with diabolically prurient intent. A soft squeeze of one breast, a healthy stroke of his fingertips on the inside of her thigh, enough to send a riot of pleasure to her very core, were only a couple of things that registered beyond the tantalizing taste of his lips. Her unintended responses included several moans of surprised pleasure that she hoped he appreciated.

As she suspected from the first time she'd seen him, Zak was very good at seduction.

His wide shoulders and sexy body covered her completely. Even if a camera was rolling non-stop somewhere in the room, no angle could capture where he touched her. She didn't want to playact anymore. She wanted him to really have sex with her.

One palm cupped her breast, only the thin knit dress separating their skin. His thumbnail stroked across her nipple, sending wild sensation straight to her moistening inner walls. His other hand found the hem of her slutty dress and pushed the fabric upward. His palm slid along her outer thigh until it reached her panties. From there his hand moved between her legs, fingertips brushing along the slim strip of fabric, stroking her perfectly across her hottest button as if he'd been there one hundred times before.

They both knew he hadn't.

She moaned as his finger continued to work magic between her legs. He pinched her nipple, sending another desperate signal to below that sex was imminent. She couldn't wait. He pulled his mouth from hers and stared down into her heated face as he touched her more intimately than any other before him.

"You're really wet." He sounded surprised.

"Of course I am." Did he not understand what two weeks of repressed lust stoked by staring at his perfect ass could do?

His tone softened as he said, "Interesting."

"Why?"

"Thought we were just putting on a show," he whispered, pressing a soft kiss to the side of her face.

"Not about our attraction."

"What makes you think I'm attracted to you?" he asked, amusement lacing the words.

The excited thrumming in her body stopped stone cold. She moved her hands to his chest and pushed him off of her. He stumbled back half a step. "Are you just faking this to get rid of me?"

He cleared his throat. His eyes roamed around the ceiling for half a second before he pierced her with a deeply serious stare. *Shit*. They were supposed to be pretending to be lovers for whatever surveillance was in the room. She'd forgotten. He *was* playacting. She wanted to have sex with him however she could get it. He was doing such a great job of seducing her. Obviously, she didn't have the experience to pull this off. She was about to get them killed.

"No. I'm not faking this just to get rid of you," he whispered loudly. "Just look down if you want to see how I *really* feel." Her gaze fell to the outline of his large cock clearly defined behind the fly of his jeans.

"Oh!" Scorching shame filled her from the top of her head to the soles of her feet. "I'm...I...didn't...expect..."

He moved back into her personal space, touched her face with a gentle caress of his fingertips, and then she forgot pretty much everything else.

"Pretend it's just the two of us together and no one else, okay?" he whispered.

Half a breath later, his mouth covered hers, his tongue licking inside. He squeezed her breast, thumb teasing her nipple. Unfortunately, his other hand didn't resume stroking between her thighs. Instead he grabbed her waist, rubbing his palm up and down her side.

Kaitlin slipped her arms around his neck. She moved her legs apart, sliding her ankle around the back of his calf, opening herself to him.

His thigh nestled between her open legs as if he couldn't help himself. His hard cock pressed deliciously into her body. He thrust himself against her a couple of times as if responding to the simple instinct to mount at every opportunity.

He's only making it look good for the camera. Kaitlin wanted him to penetrate her, or at the very least put his fingers back down between her legs.

The hand on her waist suddenly moved to cup one butt cheek. He pulled her up and then into his groin with decided force, also putting the thick, hard part of him between her legs. She tightened her grip around his neck. Their kiss had become ravenous, both of them moaning with each connected movement.

Once again his hand found a way beneath her dress, stroking along her inner thigh, pushing against the fragile fabric of her panties, now saturated with her unruly lust.

His finger slid beneath the elastic edge, zeroing in on the one place she couldn't resist having him touch. She held her breath in mid kiss, sending mental permission for him to please stroke her.

And he did. Once. Twice. The third time she almost lost it, but clamped down on her passion. She didn't want this extraordinary union to be over so quickly.

Zak kissed the corner of her mouth, disengaging the

decadent previous kiss. He brushed her cheek once with his lips. He kissed her collarbone, trailing a few more kisses to the top of her exposed breast.

She held her breath again. Head back against the door, eyes closed as he trailed kisses over her body, Kaitlin hoped this would either last forever, or that they'd be able to do it again and again in the privacy of her bedroom. Or his. Or absolutely anywhere as long as they just performed this remarkable sexy dance again.

Without a hint of his intention, Zak tugged at the neckline of her stretchy knit dress. She opened her eyes in time to see him pull the fabric down until one breast popped out. She inhaled deeply, nearly climaxing when he put his mouth around her exposed nipple and sucked it between his warm lips. She could only imagine his wide shoulders hid her brief nudity from cameras that could be anywhere in the room.

"Oh. My. Goodness." Her head tilted back and hit the surface of the door with a thud. She writhed in so much pleasure she hardly knew how to process all of the amazing sensations coursing through her.

His finger resumed stroking beneath her panties. Just when she got used to the stimulation, he stopped and slid two of his fingers inside her. She thumped her head against the door again, harder this time, when his thumb grazed her intimately as his fingers moved in and out of her wet body.

If they were being filmed, there would be no doubt that he was sucking on her breast and making her writhe in passion with his hand between her thighs. And she didn't give a flying fig.

The appeal of sex became very clear. She hadn't even seen his cock yet, and she already craved the feel of it inside her. His fingers moved in and out of her body. His thumb stroked her clit until she was on the ragged edge of pre-orgasm.

His teeth captured her nipple, exerting the most delicious pressure. At the exact same instant, his thumb stroked her with perfect pressure and his wide fingers penetrated her body just a little deeper. She exploded with a climax so intense she almost forgot to breathe. She shuddered. She groaned. When the intensity waned, her entire body trembled with shocks of the most exquisite pleasure in the aftermath of perfection.

He released her nipple, kissing his way to her mouth once more. She licked so forcefully between his lips, she surprised herself. He kissed her hard in return, hugged her tight with one arm, and slowly pulled his fingertips from between her quivering thighs.

His next move was to make it look like he fumbled with his fly, and then push his hips forward hard and fast like he'd just mounted her. He proceeded to press himself against her for quite a long time, as if ensuring his own pleasure before releasing her. He kept his face buried at her throat, kissing and licking her neck repeatedly. Unseen by the cameras, they remained fully clothed below the waist. Each time he pressed his cock against her body, she stifled her disappointment that it wasn't truly happening and held him tighter. Her arousal level started heading back up.

As much as she wanted the sex to truly be taking place, she wouldn't risk their lives for it. Zak's movements increased in tempo. He groaned loudly and froze against her as though climaxing. His unspent cock felt hard as iron between her thighs, and she had to fight the urge to rub against him. He moved his head and kissed her mouth as he pretended to refasten his pants.

As they kissed, Zak shifted the neckline of her dress into place so her breast wasn't hanging out. She honestly didn't care, but let him straighten her clothing anyway. Walking back through the bar with her moist, sucked on breast hanging out after pretending to have sex likely wasn't a good idea given the rowdy crowd she'd met upon entering.

Zak didn't need to fight any more battles for her tonight. He'd done quite a lot, and yet she wanted him for one last task.

Even with her virginity firmly in place, Kaitlin felt different. As if she'd somehow been branded by the intense gratification of Zak bringing her off.

"Will you come home with me right now?" she asked with quiet urgency. "Please." She hated to sound desperate, but she was. She wanted him to make love to her. Not in the back room of a dirty bar, but in her bedroom, on her soft sheets, within reach of the set of three condoms she'd procured while out of town for a luncheon a week ago. Way back when she fantasized about inviting her new neighbor over for dinner, hoping it would ultimately lead to her bedroom, but hadn't had the nerve to follow through.

"You know I want to, baby. But I need to go finish my business with Demarco. I've kept him waiting long enough." *Right. Mr. Demarco. Pressing bad boy business.* She shouldn't even try to persuade him any further. He'd already gone way above and beyond the call of duty. But in the afterglow of her first climax with a man making it happen, she was giddy. She wanted more. And she wanted it now.

Kaitlin didn't know what on earth came over her, but she reached between them and slid her fingers around his rigid cock, squeezing until he groaned with the sound of vivid dark pleasure.

"I'll do whatever you want. Any position you name," she whispered earnestly.

"Don't tempt me." He fairly growled his response. He put his hand on hers, covering his oversized bad boy package, but didn't pull her away. He'd pretended to climax, but he hadn't really.

She squeezed him again, wanting so much to please him the way he'd pleased her. Plus, she'd never had her fingers wrapped around a cock before. At least not willingly.

Once on a horrid date, the man she'd been with had grabbed her hand and pressed it to his crotch. The stiff finger-sized offering she'd touched long ago wasn't even in the same league as Zak's huge, rigid dick. She squeezed him again, wanting his cock inside her as she experienced the next incredibly satisfying orgasm. She made a hungry sound at the thought.

Zak pressed his forehead to hers. "You make me forget myself."

"You make me so crazy that I'm always going to want more."

He lowered his lips to hers and kissed her with a tenderness she wasn't expecting. Rubbing his lips across hers, stopping to kiss her bottom lip, her top lip, each corner of her mouth before starting over, he made her feel cherished.

Kaitlin was so touched she almost uttered the three words certain to send him packing.

I love you. How foolish. She barely knew him, but their intimate contact had a profound impact on her. She almost said those three words anyway. She meant them. She did love him. For saving her. For bringing her the most amazing pleasure she'd ever known. For not being a total bastard when she foolishly chased him into the bar tonight.

Zak smiled against her lips. He whispered, "I'll always want more, too."

In the next second, someone rattled the doorknob near her hip, and a force like a blast hit her back. The door came open about an inch. Someone wanted inside the room they occupied. And they wanted in right now!

CHAPTER 6

Zak saw the door fairly shake in its frame. He grabbed Kaitlin away from it just as Demarco burst into the room. His cock was as hard as a granite rolling pin, but began to relax when he saw the expression on Demarco's face. He looked...disturbed, for lack of a better term. He'd never seen Demarco look anything but batshit crazy because he was *always* the man to be feared in any situation.

Demarco scanned them with the briefest of looks, and then said urgently, "You have to go! Now!" In one arm, he carried the coat Kaitlin had been wearing when she entered the bar.

"What's going on?" Zak asked, pulling Kaitlin in front of him to conceal his slowly softening dick. The last thing he wanted was for Demarco to suspect the sex show had been a sham.

"Nothing you need to worry about. Both of you get out of my bar. Now!"

"Wait a minute—"

Demarco held up his palm. "You can come back tomorrow at the same time." He glanced at Kaitlin. "Come alone, and we'll discuss our business. For now, you must go."

Zak mentally shook his head. *What the fuck?*

He should be grateful that Demarco was letting him leave without signing a blood oath with regard to Kaitlin showing up as a possible witness. But the man looked seriously unnerved. Or frightened. *Pfft.* Demarco wasn't afraid of anyone, was he? If he was, perhaps Zak needed to discover who *that* someone was.

Back to the first thing again, he needed to get Kaitlin home safely. Then he'd sneak back to see who had scared this powerful man so badly.

"Fine. Tomorrow I'll be here at the same time, and I will come alone."

"Yes. Leave by way of the back entrance." He handed Kaitlin her coat.

Zak watched him exit the room without looking back. Lacing his fingers with Kaitlin's, Zak tugged her toward the door. She resisted, pulling her hand away just long enough to put on her coat.

As they came through the office door and into the pool table area, Zak noticed a tall, well-built man with two even taller, more burly guys following him step into the archway from the entry area. Their focus was turned away from where he and Kaitlin stood, thankfully.

Zak hustled Kaitlin down the short hallway, out the back door and into the chilly evening, hoping the strangers hadn't seen him or that he'd been with Kaitlin.

He didn't know who the man was, but he recognized one of his associates. This was a new wrinkle in his previously well-thought-out plans. *Fuck.* Why did everything have to be so complicated?

"What was that all about?" Kaitlin asked. The stench of the nearby garbage bins wafted toward his nose, forcing the next two breaths to come through his mouth.

"I don't know, but let's get out of here while we have the chance." What he *should* do was send her home alone then sneak back inside to listen in on whatever was going down. Probably not feasible anyway. He didn't want to leave Kaitlin alone tonight for a variety of reasons.

He wanted her with a desperation he hadn't felt in...well, forever. He should make sure she got home safely. He should also ensure that there was no fallout with regard to her being at the bar. Or what he'd done with her in the back room. Like video of it.

The musky scent of her pleasure still coated his fingertips, reminding him acutely of where he'd *just* been, what he'd *just* been doing, and how much he *absolutely* wanted to do it again.

It would be foolish to pursue her. Then again...

As they rounded the corner, he caught a glimpse of someone coming out the back door behind them. Was Demarco sending someone to see where they went? Did he want to make certain Zak wasn't lying to him about Kaitlin? Or perhaps he'd sent someone to ensure Zak didn't stay behind and eavesdrop, which was exactly what he had planned to do before dismissing it.

Either way, a shadow meant they'd have to keep playing at being a couple. He moved her in front of him in an effort to shepherd her along faster. He hoped she was interested in staying with him for a while longer. Given how forceful she'd been in the back room, perhaps her *interest* in furthering their fake relationship was the least of his worries. She'd followed him here. She'd been about to knock on his door with blueberry muffins, and when he'd rebuffed her, she'd chased after him.

The girl obviously had goals.

"What happens now?" she asked.

"You get in your car and drive home." Zak saw a

stretch limo parked directly in front of the bar's double entry door. Demarco's visitor must be someone rich and important. The closest limo service was over thirty miles away, in a larger town. His thoughts in that direction ceased when Kaitlin stopped walking and he stepped into her.

She turned and stared hard at him, vulnerability clear on her face. "Are you coming, too?" Her tone suggested urgency. Hadn't he taken the edge off for her just a few minutes ago? Maybe he needed to try harder. His cock stirred again, wanting in on any forthcoming action this time and not just a pretend session guaranteed to turn his balls a deeper shade of blue.

"Yes. I'll meet you there." Zak looked over his shoulder to see how far away their shadow was. He made out the figure of a man standing in the darkness at the corner of the building, possibly close enough to hear what they were saying.

Zak got them moving again. She asked, "Will you come to my house?" Kaitlin, of course, didn't realize they were being followed. Should he tell her? No. Better not.

He stopped by his bike, took her face in his hands, kissed her like it might be the last time they'd ever do so and said, "My only question is whether you want to sleep in my bed tonight or yours."

She sucked in a deep breath as if surprised. He was a little surprised himself. This wasn't typical protocol, but once they both disappeared into his house, maybe the follower Demarco had dispatched would be satisfied and report back in kind.

A slow, seductive smile appeared on her sweet face. "Depends," she said softly.

"On what?"

"Are you cooking breakfast, or am I?"

"I will."

"Then your place would be fine."

He kissed her tenderly once more and pressed his forehead to hers. "I'll meet you there."

"Do you promise?" she asked, uncertainty coating her question.

"No. Promises are for little girls and virgins. So I *swear* that I'll follow you." He grinned.

"Where is your car?" He knew what she drove, but didn't see her vehicle nearby.

She pointed a thumb over one shoulder at a large SUV with jumbo tires. "On the other side of that monster truck."

He walked her to her car, wanting to tuck her inside it and get her on her way. She kissed him quite passionately three times before getting into the driver's seat.

She drove away before he even got on his motorcycle. He put his helmet on, casually watching for the person following them. He couldn't tell who it was, but planned to give them a show.

Although he'd lied about having a condom in his wallet, because he always carried one, he did have a bigger box in his bedside drawer. Not that he'd had the opportunity to use any yet. Tonight he'd use half the box, given the chance.

Perhaps he could talk her into only staying with him overnight to cement the perception of them as a couple. He shouldn't have sex with her. It wasn't professional, and he didn't want to hurt her feelings when the job was done and he had to leave. But if she was determined, and she seemed to be, he'd consider it.

Having a surprise, bogus girlfriend in his life did have its perks.

Arousal pulsed through Kaitlin's body with every

breath she took. The memory of the wild ride in the dingy back room didn't make her the least bit ashamed. Somehow the thought of going to Zak's place to have more sex made the whole evening that much more exciting.

She couldn't wait to see the inside of his house. What bedroom had he chosen? She'd been in the house before Mrs. Waverly had rented it to him.

There were two bedrooms upstairs and a large bathroom in between them. Had he chosen the room on the side that looked down into her backyard? Had he ever seen her there? Had he ever watched her?

She hoped he'd chosen that bedroom *and* that he'd spied on her. Then she wouldn't be the only voyeur in this relationship. Although, she supposed, it was hardly a relationship. Sexual adventure?

Kaitlin pulled into their shared driveway and parked her car where she always did. She locked it, and strolled over to Zak's front porch to wait. *Please don't stand me up.*

A minute later, she heard the roar of his motorcycle headed her direction.

He parked in his usual spot. She didn't have a good a line of sight to his ass from her perch on his front porch, but figured that in very short order she'd get an even better view. What would his *naked* ass look like? Her heart skipped a beat. Bare perfection, likely.

She watched him pull off his helmet and dismount from a new angle. He still looked amazing.

"Thanks for not making me wait," she said as he approached.

Zak took the front porch steps two at a time to stand before her. He stared at her for a long while then a subtle smile shaped his lips. He shrugged. "I've made enough mistakes on this porch for one night. Besides, I swore I'd follow you here."

In the background noise of the night, Kaitlin heard the roar of another motorcycle nearby.

Zak glanced over his shoulder, frowning as he moved into her personal space. She slung an arm around his waist, pressing herself close. He smelled so incredible. She swore her panties got a little more saturated with each inhale. She put her cheek against his chest. He led her to his front door.

The sound of the other motorcycle got closer as he unlocked the door and brought her into his house. The scent of him surrounded her like a blanket the moment they were ensconced inside his domain.

He paused on the threshold to kiss her like he planned to keep her busy through the night. It was long moments before he closed the door to all the sounds outside. He wrapped his arms around her body, hugging her tight to his muscular frame. Even with her fuck-me heels lifting her up, her face rested just below his collarbone. She squeezed him even tighter. He dropped a kiss on the top of her hair.

"I truly am sorry I left you on my porch earlier." His deep voice rumbled deliciously through her body when he spoke.

"I'm sorry I followed you into the bar. I didn't think past my own—" she stopped speaking abruptly, unwilling to say the few obvious words that would complete her sentence. Desires. Wants. Needs.

"Shall I fill in the blank for myself?" he asked. He sounded amused, but at least he didn't laugh at her.

Kaitlin lifted her head from his chest to look him straight in the eye. "I'd really like you to fill me. Or if that's not clear enough for you, please take me to bed. I don't want to pretend this time." His cock pulsed against her hip as if in response to her words.

"My bedroom's upstairs. On the right." *The one that*

overlooks my backyard. Had he ever seen her out there? Did he watch her as scrupulously as she watched him? Did he have any inkling that she was still a virgin, desperately hoping *not* to be one very soon?

Kaitlin squeezed his waist one last time, released him and moved toward the wooden staircase centered in the entryway. She climbed to the second floor with Zak close on her heels. The bedroom door was partly open. She stepped inside where his unique male scent was very concentrated. Another pulse of moisture coated her panties.

The room seemed very tidy. The bed was made, but she didn't have a chance to study much more than that. The moment she crossed the threshold, he pulled her back against his chest. His hands suddenly roamed everywhere, from thighs to collarbone, squeezing and rubbing all her most sensitive places. His scratchy few days' growth of whiskers brushed along the back of her neck with hypnotic and seductive force as pleasure streaked down her spine with each touch.

His hands caught fistfuls of her slutty dress and drew it over her head and off, leaving her only in saturated panties and do-me black heels. He spun her around to face him, like they were a dance couple in the finals of a contest. His gaze started at her eyes, but quickly moved south. Suddenly insecure, she put her hand across her chest. He grabbed her fingers and gently urged them away to reveal her body.

"Don't ever cover up. You're so beautiful."

She shrugged, having never felt very beautiful. Typically, men never noticed her. Tonight in the bar had been a unique experience. Even the unwanted attention had been surprising, in retrospect. She had attributed their response to her extra make up and lack of a bra. Kaitlin was just glad she'd gone home with the man she'd sought out.

He kissed her softly at first, then with increasing ardor. His hands fastened on her breasts, bringing pleasure with every movement of his fingers over her sensitive nipples.

Zak nudged her backward until her legs hit the foot of his bed. He promptly picked her up like a gentleman about to carry her over a puddle, but instead dropped her smoothly to the surface of his bed. He followed her down only when he'd removed his shirt, boots and jeans, shedding his clothing so quickly she barely had time to take in all that naked skin.

Clad only in boxer briefs that did not hide *anything*, he pulled her knees apart and stroked her inner thighs with the tips of his fingers as he moved forward. He bent his head to her tummy, kissing her once near her belly button, and then nibbling her flesh as he made his way up to suckle her bare breasts.

Climbing over her, Zak slid a hand from her side, pushing downward toward her ass, taking her panties off with ease. Now she only wore shoes. Did he know how wet she was for him *now*? He also just as skillfully removed his shorts. Naked, he was magnificent. No words she'd ever read in any book did him justice.

She lifted one foot. "Aren't you going to take my shoes off?"

He grinned at her devilishly. "Nope. I like them right where they are." Zak kissed the top of her arched foot before wrapping her leg around his waist. He pressed his nude, hard, buff body into hers, and she swore she was about to faint from the excitement. *Stay awake! Don't miss this.*

The trivial concern of whether it would hurt when he pressed his huge cock inside her virgin body rose unexpectedly. This was, after all, her very first time. She shoved the trepidation aside and intently took in every sound, every scent, every view, putting this moment to memory. *My first time will be awesome.*

He stopped kissing her to reach out and pull open the drawer of his nightstand. He procured a condom packet from a large, previously unopened box, she noted, ripped it open and rose on his knees to roll the device over his huge cock.

"Like what you see?" he asked, finishing his task quickly and bending to kiss her mouth.

"Yes." *Will it hurt too much?*

"Are you ready for me?"

No. "Yes. Of course, I am."

His head twisted to one side slowly, like maybe he could read her mind. His gaze bored a hole through her. "Because if you're having second thoughts, now is the time to voice them. Once my cock is buried inside of you, I may not be able to stop until the obvious happens." A wolfish grin appeared. He looked so amazingly good. His lust-filled gaze made another gush of arousal pulse between her legs.

If he stops right now, you'll still be a virgin when Brooke arrives tomorrow.

She reached out a hand and stroked his arm. "Trust me. I can't wait to feel you inside of me."

"Okay then." He slowly lowered himself, settling his hips between her legs, pressing the tip of his cock against the opening of her body. He kissed her again, starting tender but torqueing up the passion. Soon he was devouring her. He was good at it, too.

Zak licked between her lips, distracting her with a soulful, beautiful kiss as he shifted his hips and the tip of his cock brushed her intimately. She readied herself. This was it.

One of his hands dropped to her outer thigh as if for leverage. He thrust inside her with one swift push until he was shoved fully, deeply, wholly within her slick, tight virginal body. He filled her to the brink and he was huge.

She sucked in a deep breath and arched her back as extreme pleasure touched with the barest hint of pain at being breached the first time engulfed her.

CHAPTER 7

"Holy fuck, you're tight." Zak wasn't certain if he said the words out loud or merely let them bounce around in his brain. He pulled out partway after his first thrust and heavily pushed his cock back inside Kaitlin's lovely body, hoping he'd last more than two strokes before losing control. "You feel practically virginal." Now *that* he said out loud.

Unprepared for the way she felt so amazingly snug, he also realized it had been ages since he'd been horizontal with a woman. Kaitlin had tested every single one of his built-in restraints since the moment he'd ditched her on his front porch.

She was very wet, but also incredibly small. A spasm contracted his cock at the sensation of the vise-hard grip of her around him. He alternately tried to gain control and understand why it felt so fucking amazing after only one thrust inside.

"I can explain," she whispered. "Don't be mad."

Despite the slow state of his current brain function, the sudden arch of her back and the shocked breath she drew the moment he thrust deep made him realize there was a distinct possibility that maybe she'd never done this before. Otherwise why did she have to explain something to him, and why might he be mad?

And then it struck him like a bolt of lightning. Zak was fully seated in the body of a woman who'd been a virgin only a second ago. And because of him, she wasn't anymore.

"Wait. Are you—?" He decided not to finish the question he didn't want to know the answer to. He started to withdraw, but her legs quickly wrapped around the backs of his thighs with surprising strength, keeping him embedded. The heels of her black fuck-me shoes dug into the top of his ass. His cock pulsed at the mental picture circling his brain of what her spiky heels digging into the tender flesh of his butt looked like. Hot. No question.

"Don't. Please don't leave. Not yet. Please." Tears welled in her eyes. Was he hurting her?

"If this is your first time, I don't want to injure you," he said lamely. His cock took the opportunity to pulse in protest at the idea of stopping this amazing feeling.

"You aren't hurting me. It's okay. It's fine."

He pushed his forehead to hers, and asked, "Why didn't you tell me?" But he figured he already knew the answer.

"Because I didn't want you to turn me down." Yup. That was the answer. He *would* have turned her down if he'd known.

His cock pulsed again with unrealized lust. He ignored its dissenting vote. *Absolutely, I would have said no.*

Before he could respond out loud, and he didn't know what he would have said anyway, she continued, "But now it's too late. It's done. Besides, I like the way you feel inside of me. I want more. Please. Please don't stop." Her pleading made his cock happy and ready to go, but Zak wasn't certain about what to do. He'd never deflowered a virgin before. For the first time in a very long time, he was *truly* out of his depth.

"How much does it hurt?"

"Hard...hardly at all." Was she lying? Did he hear stuttering shock in her tone because this was her first time or pain for the same reason?

He tried again to pull out, but her legs tightened. "Please, Zak, it's okay. Don't leave yet. Don't stop."

Zak lifted onto his elbows and stared down into her face. Twin lines of tears ran down her cheeks.

"Baby, if I'd known I would have done things differently." What would he have done? Run far, far away? Maybe. Maybe not.

She sniffed. "Like what?"

He kissed her gently, rubbing his lips across hers as his mind worked furiously to solve this problem. He wasn't certain how to either pull out or finish up without upsetting her or, worse, physically hurting her. A flash of inspiration came into his mind.

"Like this." He pushed his hand between their bodies and found her clit with his thumb. He stared deeply into her eyes, rubbing slowly, steadily, not planning to stop until she came apart in his arms like she had in the back room of the bar. Had that only been an hour ago?

If he gratified her, then when he moved his cock again, either to leave or finish, she'd be distracted by more pleasure and she'd also be more lubricated.

She pushed out a breath of surprise, but it didn't take long for her to loosen her legs a bit. His cock wanted to move. Zak pulled out just a little, making his hip movements small and slow, in and out, but never stopping his thumb from stroking.

Her hands moved to his ass, her nails digging in as if she wanted him to move faster, but he wasn't going to change the tempo of his strokes until she came.

Although he did lower his head and kiss her lips.

Seemingly distracted, she kissed him back, and soon her body was moving rhythmically beneath him. Her breaths increased as each push of his tongue matched the steady, small thrusts of his cock—until she climaxed, breaking the kiss, her drawn-out sigh signaling the coming squeezes of her inner walls against his cock.

With monumental effort, Zak kept the unhurried pace of his hips up even after she came, withdrawing and pushing inside, slow and deep, once, twice, thrice. He trembled on the verge of a stupendous climax. A dozen or so more thrusts pulled the phenomenal orgasm from him with clarity and a rush of pleasure so intense, his vision was impacted for a few seconds.

"Jesus," he whispered. He then growled, fucking her for several more strokes as he came down off quite an amazing release. When he finally stopped, he remained buried all the way inside of her, hoping she was okay, because he couldn't move.

After several seconds of breathing hard, Zak grabbed her close and rolled to his back, taking her with him. Her cheek pressed against his chest, but she remained silent.

"Is it time to have another discussion?" he asked.

"No."

He laughed. She relaxed against him. He was so satisfied he couldn't tense up if he had to.

"Are you okay?"

She pressed her lips to his chest. "I'm better than okay."

"Really?"

"I feel like I should thank you."

Zak pushed out a huff of disbelief. "I feel like I owe you an apology."

Her head lifted up. She stared deeply into his gaze. "Was it terrible? Was I...terrible?"

His hand came up to her face. He returned her intent

gaze. "No! For me it was fucking awesome. I'm still trying to process the shock."

"Shock?"

"I've never been anyone's first time before."

"Oh."

After several seconds, she whispered, "I thought it was awesome, too." Looking entirely too satisfied for the poor performance he'd just delivered, Kaitlin laid her head back on his chest.

"I was the one who was terrible," he said, stroking his fingertips down her back. He usually had much more stamina and self-control.

Her head came back up again. "Why would you say that?"

He laughed. "Baby, I swear to you that I truly can last longer than a dozen or so strokes before losing it."

She pondered that for a few minutes. "Well, I thought it felt amazing."

"With that first stroke I hurt you. I know I did." The acid in his belly returned.

"Only a little at first. And honestly, I was just surprised at how completely filled up I was. Having you all the way inside of me is quite a unique feeling. It was so much better than I expected. So much more overwhelming than I was prepared for."

"I hope that's true."

"It is. Plus, you're huge."

He smiled. "Thanks. I'm maybe above average, but it's nice of you to say that."

"Best I've ever had."

That spurred another laugh. "I'm the *only* one you've ever had. My manly pride makes me feel like I need to prove it to you that I have better staying power."

She grinned. "Okay."

"Not a good idea."

"Why not?"

"I don't want you to limp tomorrow."

She laughed. "I won't limp."

"How do you know?"

"I just do."

His cock pulsed to life. He rolled her to one side, kissed her soundly one more time, and climbed out of bed, heading to his bathroom to clean up.

"Hurry back." Her tone was a little bit sassy.

"Yes, ma'am." Zak hurried. Once he was staring at himself in the chest-high bathroom mirror, he also lifted his arms over his head and stretched his long frame, satisfied in the way only good sex could accomplish.

Feeling rather like a corrupter of innocents and a deplorable minuteman missile lover all at the same time, Zak talked himself into one more round of sexual decadence tonight to feed her curiosity. Likely she'd demand it, and he didn't want to fight her. He would, however, take his time. He'd last longer than a few strokes inside her incredible, newly unvirginal, tight body.

When he returned to the bedroom, Kaitlin waved. In her fingers was another condom. "I like that you have a huge supply on hand. This box looks brand new. Tell me, am I the first woman you've been with since you got to town?" Her shy smile tugged at places in his soul he should close the door on, but couldn't seem to manage.

He smiled back, climbing into bed with her. "Yes. You're the first female company I've had since I moved here."

"Really?" she asked politely, but the tone of her voice and the satisfied expression on her face suggested she already knew that. If he'd brought any women home, she would have seen it.

Zak needed to work harder to put forth his badass persona and not his real feelings about this girl and what had just happened between them. Besides, it kept the shit-heel feelings he had about using her at bay. "You ought to know that, baby. You've watched me come home each and every day. I was always alone."

She sucked in a sharp breath. "How did you—" She cut herself off.

He forced another grin, adding some bad-boy arrogance to the expression. "Because I saw your curtains move every single night that I pulled my bike into the driveway. I figured you'd come over long before you actually did."

A small smile appeared. "I guess I've been pretty obvious. And cowardly."

He lifted one shoulder. "I'd say curious." How on earth did he intend to handle this going forward? How would she *let* him handle this? As far as the criminals he was trying to put away were concerned, she was his woman. He couldn't confess to her his true identity or his non-criminal motives. Maybe if he played this right, she wouldn't need to be rolled up into the witness protection program after this was all over with Demarco.

Her gaze captured his with an intensity he found charming. "In truth, I was desperate."

His brows furrowed. "Why desperate?"

She heaved an annoyed sounding sigh. "My sister— or rather, my stepsister—is visiting me tomorrow, whether I like it or not. And I don't." Her frown shifted suddenly to a satisfied smile. "This coming visit will mark the very first time since we've been adults that she won't be able to lord it over me that she's a seasoned woman of the world with a string of perfect lovers in her history, and I'm only a hopeless virgin living temporarily in a small town without any good prospects."

Shit, more family coming? Great. Zak rolled closer and snatched the condom from her fingers, prepared to play a game of bad-boy love 'em and leave 'em. Maybe he wouldn't have sex with her again. "Oh. So you only wanted me for my stud services and only temporarily." Though that would actually be better for his cover, his tone was harsher than he'd intended.

"No. That's not what I wanted. It's not *all* I wanted." She lifted up on one elbow, her expression soulfully repentant. Her soft hand shot out, squeezing and caressing his shoulder. They stared at each other for a count of five. He didn't want to play with her after all. He really wanted to have sex with her again, as depraved as that might be. But mostly he wanted the opportunity to make it amazing for her this time. Besides, the second time didn't hurt, or so he'd heard.

She needed to be his woman for the time being. A passing thought regarding the motorcycle that had followed him home crossed his mind. Allowing a smile to shape his lips, he said, "I'm teasing, baby. I'm not offended. I'm just surprised. When you didn't come over that first week, I figured you weren't interested."

"I've been fascinated by you since the first day I saw you ride up on your motorcycle."

"And you never came over until today because…?"

She flashed another sweet smile. "I used to be a frightened virgin, fearful someone would see me ogling you and thinking impure thoughts. But things have recently changed for me."

He laughed. "So, what, now you're a woman of the world?"

"Well, I'm definitely worldlier than I was when I woke up this morning." She stared at his mouth, his eyes, his jaw, his face, softening her posture as each second ticked by. She reached out to brush her finger along his chin where a scar from his childhood was. "You are incredible."

Zak leaned forward, unable to keep his lips off her for a second longer. She kissed him back with enthusiasm. His dick roared forward with the sincere desire to fuck wildly. Nothing was between them, not even the bed sheet. He rolled on top of her, keeping their lips attached and very engaged.

Her fingertips explored the planes of his back. Her legs shifted beneath his, widening for what came next. Sex. Wanting to gain a modicum of control, he broke the kiss to use the condom in his hand instead of just clutching it abstractedly while he fucked her with abandon.

Once safely sheathed, he scooted up next to her. He put a hand between her legs and his mouth on the center of one breast. Her back arched when he sucked that hardened nipple between his lips. His cock pulsed against her leg. The thought of putting his dick inside her tight body made him want to come.

Stroking her clit a little bit faster, Zak planned to ensure she was really wet before attempting to breach her again. Doubt crept in that he shouldn't be doing this. Deflowering her was bad enough. Ensuring she was wet enough for a second hedonistic round of sex was likely depraved. But he couldn't stop. The way she gripped his shoulder, she likely wouldn't let him anyway.

Her breathing increased. She was about to go over the edge. He wanted to be inside her when she did. He shifted, covering her with his body. He released her nipple and kissed her luscious mouth, at the same time centering his hips between her thighs.

Kaitlin widened her legs to make it easier for him.

"Tell me if it hurts too much."

She smiled and nodded, but he didn't expect her to tell him anything. She wanted this almost more than he did. He pushed into her hot, tight, wet body very slowly. The smile on her lips didn't change. Her hands, gripping his shoulders, relaxed as he moved deeper and deeper.

Once he was all the way inside, Zak paused. He

looked into her eyes, searching for any hint of pain or distress. If she had any discomfort, she hid it well. "I love the way it feels when we are so…intimately connected," she whispered.

"Me, too," he whispered back.

He pulled his cock out and then pushed back inside, unhurried.

"I won't break, you know. You can go faster. You feel really great."

He nuzzled her neck. "I'm glad. But this is more about me not losing control so quickly for the second round."

"Okay."

"In fact, let's change positions."

"What?"

Zak slid his arms beneath her, hugged her tight and rolled onto his back again, his hand on her ass making sure they remained firmly connected.

Once she was on top, her expression was pensive, but not panicked or pained. She lifted up a bit. He stroked her ass a few times and then flattened his palms on her outer thighs. "Move your knees up on the bed."

Tentatively, her legs moved until her knees were on either side of his hips. She was still wearing the fuck-me shoes. His cock pulsed within her body. Her breasts were deliciously pressed to his chest. She didn't seem too sure of this new position or how good it could feel.

"Sit up," he said, pressing her shoulders back until she sat astride his hips. His cock moved as she did, pulsing in delight. She must have felt it, because she smiled at him.

"Now what?" Her breathy voice was making his *last longer than a few strokes* plan more difficult to imagine.

"Ride me." He pushed his hands beneath her bottom and lifted her a bit. "Move up and down on me at whatever speed you choose."

She looked down at the place where their bodies joined erotically, a sweet, unexpected blush filling her cheeks.

"Try it," he said.

She moved upward and promptly pushed back down, going even deeper than he'd been previously. She sucked in an appreciative breath. "I get it." Kaitlin moved her body up, allowing his cock to almost exit before impaling herself on him harder and faster than he would have done.

A grin shaped her lips. "Good. This is good." She moved again and again, her eyes wide with exuberant delight with each satisfying move.

His voice sounded gravelly to his own ears when he said, "Put your hands on the headboard. If you grip there, you'll get better leverage."

Both of her arms went over him and clutched the bars of the painted iron bed. She tested the control, moving only her hips like an elliptical machine, half up and down, half front to back. For Zak it was amazing. She grinned and moved faster.

Zak pushed a hand between them, his thumb circling her clit as she rode him. The moment he started fingering her, the faster and more satisfying her movements became. The sensation was so incredibly arousing, Zak's libido zoomed forward, ready to take a giant leap over the edge and directly into gratification. He had to clamp down and enforce some control over his desire to let go.

He pushed her clit harder, circling with even more pressure. He watched her pleasure, felt her body move against his, and heard the sexy sounds she made each time she impaled herself in him. The whole scenario made for an incredibly sensual experience.

Zak was on the very edge of losing control. He put his free hand on one dangling breast, squeezing her pert nipple between his fingers. That got a swift reaction. Kaitlin increased her speed and she was moving at a pretty good clip as it was.

Every stroke was a lesson in trying to keep his cool.

Kaitlin slammed down on his cock, stiffened all of a sudden, arching backward as a shriek issued forth. He thought it sounded like a very gratified shriek.

The telltale sign of her orgasm squeezed his already tautly compressed dick. Nirvana couldn't feel as good as virginally tight Kaitlin climaxing around his cock. Zak moved his hands to her hips and as she slowed her movements, he thrust upward two, three, four more times trying to find his own release.

The contractions of her inner walls helped the blinding arousal he felt. Ten, eleven, twelve...she felt so fucking incredible.

Her hands rested on his shoulders, squeezing with each thrust he made. After a few seconds she started whispering, "So good. So good." Over and over again.

Zak was on the edge, two strokes away. "Kaitlin. Look at me." He wanted to look into her eyes the moment he came.

Her gaze drilled into his. She looked delighted. She looked satisfied. She looked like a woman in love. Dangerous. But in the next moment he didn't concern himself with the danger of her affection. He pushed his hips upward. He came, feeling like a shower of molten shrapnel left his body in a wide, awesome spray. A few more thrusts completed his amazing journey.

Whoosh. Done. Spent.

She collapsed on his chest, her panting breaths moving across his collarbone. He tightened his arms around her, crushing her in his embrace. If he'd ever been more content after a sexual encounter, he didn't remember it.

As the pleasure of his climax receded, Zak's thoughts

went directly into *what have I done* mode. As good and relaxed as he felt right now, there would be a price for this pleasure. He hoped he had the currency to pay for it.

Zak pulled away from her, cleaned up in the bathroom and returned to bed quickly. He sensed cuddling would be in his future, and decided that wouldn't be so bad.

He hugged her close and kissed the top of her head. She stirred against him, a satisfied sound coming from her throat. Before he could think of the right thing to say, the sound of someone pounding on his door echoed up the stairs and into his room.

He tensed two seconds before detaching himself again.

"Who could that be?" Kaitlin asked drowsily.

"Don't know. I'll be back in a minute." Was it the shadow Demarco had sent? Was the guy following him going to expect to be invited in to see Kaitlin in his bed? Too fucking bad. Not going to happen.

Zak stopped only long enough to step into his boxers and jeans and grab his gun from the hiding spot in his top dresser drawer. He didn't even zip up, flying down the stairs barefoot, taking them two at a time, and hoping this wasn't about to be a showdown with anyone from the biker bar.

Hadn't he just done what was expected of him? Hadn't he just *taken care of his woman* so Demarco could conduct business with some stranger Zak needed to identify? Hadn't Demarco sent someone after him to ensure he didn't sneak back and check up on the meeting?

He pulled the door open with his best *what the fuck* expression in place to find an attractive, well-dressed woman peering at him. Her surprised expression turned to one of feline interest as she glanced down his bare chest until she reached his unzipped fly.

CHAPTER 8

"What?" Zak's clearly annoyed tone floated up to the bedroom where Kaitlin waited for him. She wanted more sex tonight. Maybe she did want to limp tomorrow.

"Hello there."

Kaitlin recognized the female voice immediately. She leapt from his bed like it had been lit on fire. She kicked off her heels as she heard, "I'm sorry to bother you. I'm Brooke Bailey. Your next-door neighbor is my sister. I tried knocking on her door, but she doesn't seem to be home, which is very unusual. Actually, I thought this was her landlady's house. Anyway, I don't suppose you know where my sister is, do you?"

Kaitlin grabbed the first article of clothing she found. It was Zak's T-shirt. She didn't even bother with panties, exiting his room and sailing down the stairs as Zak turned toward the staircase.

"I do," he said as she crashed inelegantly into his side. She noticed that he put what looked like a gun in the drawer of the table next to the front door. She noted that for a later discussion.

"Brooke," she said, out of breath. "What are you doing here?"

Her stepsister's eyes widened to practically the size of dinner plates. "Kaitlin? What...? I mean...how?" She shook her head. Her gaze pivoted sharply from Kaitlin's likely disheveled hair down the length of her near-nude body to her bare feet and back again.

"You weren't supposed to be here until tomorrow," Kaitlin said, trying to keep the accusatory tone from her voice.

Zak slid his arm around Kaitlin's waist, his fingers coming to a stop right below her breast, pulling the fabric tight and outlining her pert nipple. It was cold outside.

"Well, I..." Brooke sent her puzzled gaze to Zak again. Then to where his hand rested. He casually brushed a thumb beneath the curve of Kaitlin's breast as Brooke practically convulsed, her eyes bugging out of her head.

"Is this going to take very long, baby?" Zak asked. He looked down, meeting Kaitlin's eyes. "Because I'm not quite through with you yet."

"No, this won't take long. Go back to bed. I'll be there in a minute. I swear."

"You have exactly one minute. And I'll be timing you." He smacked one T-shirt-covered butt cheek, licked his tongue across the center of her lips once, and then pulled away, climbing up the steps chanting, "One, one-thousand. Two, one-thousand. Three..."

Kaitlin stifled a grin and turned to her stepsister, who was watching Zak's perfect ass climb the stairs. She wanted to smack the lustful look from Brooke's face, but instead asked again, "What are you doing here, Brooke? You said tomorrow."

Brooke lifted one skinny arm, pointed to the staircase and with a venomous tone said, "You cannot possibly be sleeping with him."

"You're right. We were not doing anything close to

sleeping." Kaitlin leaned a shoulder against the doorframe.

"You're fucking him?"

"That's none of your business." Kaitlin's heart pounded in her chest with a feeling of joyous pride over being free from her virginity, and the satisfaction of seeing her stammering stepsister's reaction. "What is your problem?"

Brooke seemed to collect her poise with effort. "Well, I've come all this way. Aren't you going to invite me in?"

"No. This isn't my house. Come back tomorrow morning, over there." She pointed at her house. "As you can see, I'm busy tonight. If you'd called to tell me your plans had changed, you'd know that already."

Brooke's expression, set somewhere between aghast and horrified, brought Kaitlin back to earth. She pushed out a breath. Perhaps she was being a bad hostess.

From the stairwell, she heard Zak call out clearly, "Twenty-five, one-thousand. Twenty-six, one-thousand…"

No. She was not being unfair or a bad hostess. Her sister should have called and not just expected her to be able to change her plans on a whim. Kaitlin wasn't changing her current plans. She was going back to Zak's bed.

"Listen. I've got to go. You're on your own." She didn't try to suppress the foolish grin she couldn't stop.

Brooke huffed. "You could at least let me stay at your house. The taxi I came here in is already gone." Her gaze wandered up toward where Zak continued to count audibly.

Kaitlin wanted in the worst way to tell her to get a motel, but a life filled with manners stopped her. "All right. Fine. You can stay there. I have an extra key under the right-side flower pot next to the backdoor window."

She pointed to the gate door separating the two houses. "You know where the spare bedroom is. You can make up the bed. Sheets are folded on the mattress."

Brooke glanced up the stairs again. She cleared her throat. "When will you be home?"

Kaitlin, unused to this sudden change in the balance of power between them, almost buckled in the face of her stepsister's sullen expression. *Be strong.*

"Not sure. Sometime in the morning, maybe."

"Don't you have to work?"

"No. I took the day off to get ready for *your* arrival *tomorrow afternoon.*"

Brooke frowned. "My plans changed very suddenly. I didn't have time to call you." With no apology offered, Kaitlin was feeling less and less magnanimous.

"Be that as it may, if you want to stay at my house tonight, you'll have to make your own bed. Or you can find a bed elsewhere. It's your choice."

Her stepsister sniffed in that infuriatingly snotty way she had when one of her whims wasn't met. She wanted to shift the course of the conversation to her advantage. Kaitlin wasn't going to let her. She reached for the edge of the door to close it.

"Wait!" Brooke's eyes went wide again. She looked at Kaitlin more closely. "Who is this guy? I mean, you're wearing his T-shirt and nothing else, for heaven's sake."

"Good night, Brooke." She closed the door halfway.

"Kaitlin Jane Price!"

"Don't say my middle name."

"Stop acting like some sex kitten that I know you aren't."

"You don't know me at all, Brooke."

"I'm going to tell Mom and Dad that you're fucking around with a criminal."

"Go ahead. I'm an adult. And for the record, he's not

a criminal." *I hope.* Kaitlin slammed the front door shut, already regretting telling her stepsister where her spare key was and hoping Zak hadn't heard a single word of their conversation.

She engaged the deadbolt, turned and marched up the stairs, anger rolling through her in waves. Brooke was going to be difficult for this whole visit, as usual. How dare she issue threats? Zak was none of her business.

Kaitlin marched into Zak's bedroom, seething. Then she saw him. He waited for her, reclining on his back in the very center of the bed. The sheets were tangled beneath him. His hands were folded behind his head, and his expression was hard to read. But the only thing she really noticed was that he was still wearing his jeans, although he'd taken the liberty of zipping them up. She stopped in her tracks, wondering how to get those jeans unzipped and off him.

"You're still wearing your pants," she said.

"And you're still wearing my shirt," he replied easily.

"Want it back?" she asked. "I sort of thought we weren't done yet. At least I hope we're not."

Zak shrugged, a lazy smile shaping his lips. "Now that you've told your stepsister off, and she can't possibly believe you're a virgin any longer, I wonder if you even need me anymore."

"I do."

"What for?"

I'm not ready to be done yet. I want more. "Experience?"

He frowned. "Meaning what?"

She took a step closer to the edge of the bed. "Well, there are a few more positions I'd like to familiarize myself with in a practical sense."

"Such as?"

Kaitlin pressed her fingers together, knotting them briefly. "Have you ever heard the term doggie-style?"

His cock moved, stiffening before her very eyes. She could see the shape of it under the fly of his jeans.

His hands moved from behind his head, sliding his body closer to where she stood. She took another step forward. Zak sat up, dropped both legs off the side of the bed, pulled her between his knees and pressed the side of his head to her breasts. "Let me be very clear. There will be no more sex tonight."

"But why?" Her hands rested on his shoulders, but she smoothed them down his muscular back, loving the feel of him.

He tilted his head to stare into her eyes. "You may not be a virgin any longer, but it's been less than an hour since that happened. Not to mention we went two rounds already. You need to recuperate for longer than ten minutes before making your way through the rest of the Kama Sutra positions."

"Please. I'm fine. I don't hurt." *Much.*

"Liar."

"Okay, maybe I'm not ready for this night to be over yet." Kaitlin resisted the urge to whine and beg him for more. "I'm afraid it might be the only one I ever get and I'm taking advantage of all I can acquire."

Zak pushed out a long sigh. "I'm not fucking you again, Kaitlin. I don't care what words you use to tempt me."

Kaitlin was pushing her luck. Reviewing her evening, she'd gathered her courage, made the first move, been pushed aside, followed the object of her desire, nearly involved herself in a possibly shady deal in a biker bar, planned another liaison, allowed herself to be taken to bed for the first time, lost her virginity, experienced more orgasms in a single night than all of the last month, and now pouted because he wouldn't take her a third time, as he somehow knew she *was* feeling a bit raw inside.

She'd tempted him with the term doggie-style and he'd denied her. A smile surfaced. She had another term.

"What about a blowjob?"

"Fuck," he whispered.

"Want one?"

"Have you ever done it before?"

"No. But you can teach me. I promise, I'm a fast learner."

Zak's shoulders felt tense under her hands. His cock throbbed against her leg.

She pressed her palm against the front of his jeans, and his growing erection.

"At least your cock is interested."

He didn't move. "My cock isn't the only one interested, but we should cool it down for the evening."

"Why?" She wanted to at least try it once. She figured if she got started, perhaps he'd tell her what to do to finish.

Falling to her knees, Kaitlin put her hands on his fly, intent on releasing his glorious cock to her view. He stopped her, covering her fingers with both hands.

"You might not need to work in the morning, but I do. I need to get some sleep."

"I forgot you heard my stepsister and me." Kaitlin sucked in a breath. "What else did you hear?"

"Everything. You were both shouting, *Kaitlin Jane Price.*"

She closed her eyes, shoulders slumping a bit. She hated her middle name. Plain Jane.

"Don't kick me out." She lifted her gaze to his. "Please."

"I'm not kicking you out. I'm going to take my jeans off, slide into bed and sleep very soundly. You can stay here with me if you plan to sleep. You can even wear my T-shirt."

Kaitlin nodded. He shucked his jeans off, watching

her warily, as if she'd corrupt him any second given the chance. He was right. She would.

"I wasn't any good, was I?" Her insecurity about her lack of experience roared forward in the wake of his refusal to go a third round.

"What?"

"At sex. You can tell me. I can take it."

He grabbed her hands. "That's not true."

"But—"

"But nothing. Listen. I won't lie. I enjoyed it. But this wasn't in my plans. I'm not looking for a steady girlfriend, but now I'm saddled with one."

"What?"

"Demarco expects us to be a couple. I hoped not to involve you in that business any more than you already are, but the truth is, it would be the height of suspicious to break up with you after the kind of public spectacle we put on tonight at his place. You've put me in a very difficult position with less than superior people."

"I'm sorry," she said quietly. She hadn't stopped to consider his issues. Her gaze dropped to his chest. "But what do you mean suspicious?"

He pushed out a long breath. "Never mind that. I'm not sorry. But while I didn't expect to acquire a girlfriend, we'll need to pretend that we're together for the next few days, maybe longer."

Kaitlin nodded. "Okay."

"How long will your stepsister stay?"

She shrugged. "Two days, possibly three. I'm not certain of her plans. She rarely lets me know her schedule in advance."

"Can you get rid of her tomorrow?"

"Doubtful, but I'll try. She's not easy to control or tell what to do."

"So that runs in the family then?" He smiled, so she did too. He was right. She'd been pushy.

"Touché." Perhaps she had learned that from Brooke. It always garnered her exactly what she wanted. To be fair, it had also helped Kaitlin get what she wanted tonight. Perhaps she did need to be more like her sister in some respects.

"Tell her she's cramping our style."

"Will she be?" Kaitlin asked wistfully.

He gave her a heated stare, but didn't answer. He turned and pulled the sheets down, gesturing for her to get into bed. She did.

She scooted to the far side and turned away from him. They may have had phenomenal sex, but they were not a couple. They were only pretending to be involved. Then again, it was difficult to feel anything but gratified, regardless of the temporary nature of their awkward relationship.

Zak climbed into bed and turned the bedside lamp off. To her surprise, he spooned against her back, molding his perfect body to hers. He kissed the nape of her neck, draping one arm possessively over her hip.

"Good night," he murmured. "Sleep tight."

Kaitlin didn't move. His even breathing started seconds later.

She relaxed against him and closed her eyes, but wasn't a bit tired. Kaitlin focused on the vast memories of her day, reliving the time at the bar and her time here with Zak, cataloging goals achieved tonight.

Odious virginity gone. Check.

More than one sexual position experienced. Check.

Kissed like she'd always wanted to be, multiple times. Check.

Shock her stepsister, Brooke. Check.

Fall in love with a man she couldn't have. Checkmate.

CHAPTER 9

The sun hadn't risen yet, but Zak woke at dawn as usual. He'd slept like the dead, not surprising after the previous evening of amazing sexual activity. Kaitlin was spooned up against him. Had they even moved at all in the night?

He lifted his head, staring at the side of her face before carefully extracting himself so she wouldn't wake up.

Zak crept downstairs, snagged his secret private cell phone and called Miles.

Without preamble, the voice on the other end of the line answered with, "What happened last night?"

"I went to make the deal without cash in hand, but someone else showed up and scared Demarco. I got rushed out before the details were even discussed."

"Who was it?"

"I don't know. I've never seen him before, but I recognized one of his bodyguards."

"Because of your brother?"

Many of his fellow undercover associates were aware that Zak's younger brother was a very successful bodyguard. Deke had saved "very important people" on more than a few occasions. There was even talk of a reality television show at one time. Zak would rather be staked face down over an anthill smeared in raw honey. He wasn't certain how his brother felt about the TV offer.

"No. From a job I did a couple of years back. He's hired muscle to the highest bidder. But Demarco was freaked out about the visitor, and I was shuttled out quickly. I'm fairly certain none of the newcomers saw me, including the bodyguard. I'm not certain he'd recognize me anyway. But if Demarco is worried about anybody, I believe we should find out why."

"Is it worth pursuing over our stated mission plan?"

"Yes." *What the hell?*

"Is that your ego talking because you want to take Demarco down so badly?"

"No." *Maybe.*

"I know what Demarco did to your cousin." *Lots of people do.*

"That's not relevant to this case."

Miles barked, "The fuck it isn't."

"If you don't trust my judgment, why am I even here?"

"Because I got overruled." *Really? Fuck.*

"Listen. No one wants Demarco more than me, for a variety of reasons, but I swear to you, the issue of what he did to my cousin is only one in a long list of things he needs to answer for. He needs to go down. But I'm not stupid. Given the opportunity presented last night, I'd also dearly love to get the guy who makes *him* nervous."

He heard a sigh at the end of the line. "Fine. Do what you can to discover who he is and we'll discuss it. No promises of a mission change."

"Sure."

"One more thing."

"Yeah?"

"Who's the blonde?"

"What blonde?" *How the fuck does he know about Kaitlin?*

"The one you left behind upstairs in your bed."

Zak would never understand how his handler knew things he shouldn't. Perhaps he was psychic. Or more likely he had spies or hidden surveillance or both.

Zak looked at each of the four corners of the room he hunkered down in, searching for a pinhole camera. Seeing nothing, he answered slowly, "She's my next-door neighbor."

"Do I need to be worried about *her* now, too?"

"No." *Maybe.*

"You aren't very convincing."

"She followed me to the bar. That's all. She's not involved in this mission. But Demarco thinks we're a couple. I had to play it that way last night to keep her safe." He cleared his throat. "I'll likely have to continue the act for the time being."

"'The act.' As if. Now I really don't like it."

"You never like anything."

"There's a good reason for that. It's my job to be the one who doubts. Bottom line for now, do what you have to do. You will anyway. Find out the name of the man who scared Demarco and report back. Do not engage the possible new target. You got me?"

"Got it."

Zak returned the phone to its hiding place and padded to the kitchen to start a pot of coffee. He did have to go to work today. Sometimes the hardest part of these undercover missions was keeping up the charade of whatever character he was playing. This time he was the new mechanic at a local motorcycle garage where his *in* to Demarco's organization, Julio, also worked.

Mechanical work was a good fit. It came to him naturally. He'd grown up around cars. His father had instilled in all five of his sons a very good work ethic along with the idea that no job was beneath them and also that a job well done was good for the soul. He was lucky to have grown up in the family he did. He often missed his brothers when he was undercover for long stretches. His only contact with The Organization and his real life was Miles.

Would Kaitlin like the "real" Zak and his family?

He glanced upward in the direction of where she still slept, wondering what in the hell he was going to do about her. He wasn't a fool. He wouldn't get to keep her. But he wanted to.

Memories from last night invaded his mind as the first drips of coffee filled the glass carafe. In the window. In the bar. In his bed. On his cock. He shook his head, trying to dispel the vision of her well-satisfied expression directly after she climaxed while riding him. That dreamy look would live in his memory for a long while, along with her scent. Cherry vanilla would forever remind him of last night and of her.

As if conjured from his imagination, Kaitlin appeared at the kitchen door. Wearing his T-shirt, she looked sleepy, well-fucked and absolutely delicious.

"Good morning, baby. Sleep well?"

She blinked slowly, nodded and blushed vividly.

He motioned for her to join him. She shuffled across the floor, head down, perhaps napping along the way. Without looking at him, she pushed her body into his, wrapped her arms loosely around his torso and buried her face into his shoulder.

"Are you even awake yet?" he asked, planting a soft kiss on her forehead. He breathed in her unique fragrance, letting it settle into his lungs.

She shook her head. "Not until after I have a sip of coffee. That's all I need. Just a little bit of caffeine to lift my brain from the fog of slumber."

"Okay." The ancient coffee maker was loud, spitting

plumes of steam from several places as a steady stream of wakeup juice collected in the pot. "Let me make us both a cup."

She shook her head. "I'll just have a sip of yours, okay?" She squeezed his middle gently and let out a little sexy sigh.

A pulse of lust hit hard in the center of his chest at the idea of sharing his coffee with her. Why did that simple act seem so intimate? Especially after all they'd done last night.

He grabbed the carafe, much to the protest of the coffee maker, which started sputtering and shooting steam out of even more places. He managed to pour half a cup before thrusting the pot back under the still dripping source.

Zak took a quick sip of dark, rich black coffee then handed the cup to her. She sipped from the same place he did and promptly hummed as if content. He'd expected her to spit it out and request loads of creamer and sugar before drinking.

"Mmm. This is really good."

"You drink your coffee black?"

She took a deeper sip, moaning this time in appreciation. "Yes. And this is also very strong and very hot, just the way I like it best." Kaitlin took a third and final sip and handed the cup back to him, but kept her body pressed close. He finished the rest of the short cup in a single swallow.

He did have particular tastes where his morning beverage was concerned. He was gratified that *his woman* also appreciated his tastes in that arena and shared them.

"When do you have to go to work?" she asked, the breath from her words bouncing along his pecs. Her eyes seemed to brighten with a bit more awareness after the coffee she'd enjoyed, but not much.

"Soon. I've got to shower first."

"Excellent. May I join you?"

He grunted, wondering if he'd ever make it to work if they showered together.

"Is that a 'yes' grunt or a 'no' grunt?"

He pushed out a long sigh and hugged her tight, wanting to shower with her more than he wanted to be on time to work. "Come on. You can shower with me. But I don't want to be late."

"I won't make you late."

"I don't believe that for a second. Just looking at you sexy and sleep rumpled makes me want to call in sick and stay in bed all day."

"Really?" she asked, giving him a half-lidded look before burrowing her face back into his shoulder.

"Yes, really."

"That's so sweet." *I am not sweet. But you make me want to be.*

Zak poured another full cup of coffee one-handed and steered her upstairs. She was absolutely adorable. He needn't have worried about an active threat to his self-control while they showered. Even with a few sips of coffee, she seemed barely able to function.

After a quick scrub of his body and hair as she leaned against the shower stall, Zak pushed her beneath the water, soaped her body, washed her hair and rinsed her off.

Once they were clean, he considered getting her dirty again, but didn't want to hurt her after last night's premier performance.

She seemed to rouse once he toweled her dry and shoved yesterday's sexy outfit into her hands.

"Guess it's time for the walk of shame back over to my house." She slipped the black-and-red dress over her head and grabbed the fuck-me heels.

"There was nothing shameful about last night,

baby." He brushed a wet strand of her hair behind one ear.

"I wonder if the neighbors will feel that way," she said as he helped her put her coat on.

He shrugged. "It's early. You can sneak out the back if you'd like. The fence we share will shield you from the street."

"Thanks, Zak."

"My pleasure."

"Was it?" she asked, drilling a gaze deeply into his eyes.

He tilted his head to one side. "Was it what?" Where was she going with this?

She swallowed hard, her expression difficult to read but seemingly angst filled. "Did you have any pleasure?"

Zak took her face in his palms, gave her his best sexy half-smile and said quietly, "I had plenty of pleasure."

"Did you get enough that you want to be with me again, or is this all I get?"

He should boot her out and break her heart right now, but Demarco would find it suspicious. Better to stay in her life until he was certain that scumbag wouldn't bother her.

At least that was the lie he told himself to say what he wanted to say. "If you want more, I'll make myself available. I just don't want you to follow me to that bar again. Deal?"

"Deal."

"Have fun with your stepsister."

At first she grunted, but suddenly she brightened. "Thanks for that, too. I expect this to be a very interesting visit instead of dreadful like usual."

He watched as she snuck over to her back door, carrying her shoes in one hand. His barefoot virgin was safely home again.

Zak filled a thermos with the rest of the pot of coffee

and headed to the shop. Julio would likely have a few words for him today. His friend had left the bar soon after Kaitlin entered, but Zak didn't know why or where he went. He hadn't seen him when Demarco hustled them out either. He expected his day would be very interesting.

Kaitlin managed to make it all the way to her room without making a sound, only to discover that her sister hadn't bothered to make up the bed in the guest bedroom. She'd just crawled into Kaitlin's.

Furious, Kaitlin stopped being quiet, slamming her shoes on the floor one at a time. Brooke sat up in bed. *Her* bed.

"Finally back home after whoring all night?" she said, looking as alert as if she'd been waiting wide awake for Kaitlin's return.

Kaitlin didn't want to take the bait, but couldn't seem to help herself. "Why is it that when you sleep with a guy, it's exciting and something I should aspire to, but when I do it, I'm whoring all night?"

Brooke frowned.

Kaitlin crossed her arms and marched to the foot of her bed. "My question to you is why you were too lazy to make up the guest bed last night."

"I was tired after a long day of traveling."

"Is that so? And it was such a long day of travel that you couldn't possibly find two minutes to call me or text me to let me know you'd changed your plans?"

"How many more times are you going to bring that up?"

"I suspect until you leave town." Kaitlin took off her coat and hung it up.

Brooke climbed out of bed, wearing what looked like men's pajamas. "I was going to invite you to a lavish dinner with my new boyfriend tonight. I was even going to let you bring *your* sketchy love interest along, but now I'm reconsidering."

"Whatever. I don't care." She wasn't going to let her stepsister bring her down after such a perfect night with Zak.

Brooke's mouth hung open unflatteringly. Kaitlin ignored her and grabbed a fresh change of clothes, disappearing into her bathroom to dry her hair and prepare for the coming day.

When she returned, Brooke was nowhere to be seen. While she hadn't made the bed, exactly, she'd pulled the covers up to the pillows. A marvel if there ever was one.

Kaitlin pondered her options. She'd taken the day off, figuring Brooke would want to take her out for an expensive three-hour lunch and regale her with whatever was current in her very important and much more interesting life. It was the price Kaitlin paid to keep her family in her life. Not for the first time she realized she was laying out quite a premium for little in return.

Brooke sat at her kitchen table, seemingly waiting for Kaitlin. The coffee maker wasn't going yet. It was likely too much to ask for her stepsister to lift a finger to help out. The pulled up covers had probably exhausted her *assistance* for the day.

Kaitlin had already had a few sips of Zak's strong coffee. She smiled at the recollection and pondered the idea of forgoing any further morning beverage.

"I need coffee," Brooke announced in that whiny voice that made Kaitlin want to grind her back teeth together until they cracked.

"Then why didn't you start the coffee maker?" Kaitlin asked, expecting Brooke to make a face, which she did.

She rolled her eyes. "I don't know where you keep your coffee."

Kaitlin shrugged. "I already had coffee with Zak. You're on your own."

Brooke's face turned a very unflattering shade of crimson. "Are you going to be difficult for the whole time I'm here?"

"Maybe it's time you finally understood how I've felt for every single one of *your* previous visits. I get the sense that you don't like them either. So I've turned over a new leaf. I'm not your doormat any longer." Kaitlin felt somehow imbued with a new inner strength after spending the night with Zak. She'd had great sex with a bad boy, no less, and Brooke had caught her.

She tried to picture what would have happened if she hadn't followed Zak to the bar. It was an easy vision. Right now she'd be miserable, listening to Brooke go on and on about her latest boyfriend, the hot monkey sex they were having, and the priceless gems he'd bought her to add to her extensive jewelry collection.

"I don't understand." Brooke looked sincerely confused by Kaitlin's new attitude.

"Of course you don't. You live in your own world and rarely think of anyone but yourself. You're a taker, Brooke. You always have been and, worse, I've let you get away with it. But listen carefully. No more! I have a life. Yours is not better than mine. It's just different."

She'd never spoken to Brooke this way. Given Brooke's expression, it was a surprise to both of them.

"I never meant to make you feel…" Brooke paused, seeming to search for a nice word to replace the one they both knew she wanted to use. *Shitty.*

"Bullshit. You always meant to make me feel shitty and belittled. That's how you operate. I've just decided I'm not going to put up with your crap ever again. No more."

"Kaitlin!"

"I'll repeat myself, Brooke. No. More. If you want

coffee, then figure out how to use the coffee maker or go out and buy a cup. I'm going upstairs to strip my bed and wash the sheets you slept on last night because you were too lazy to make up the guest bed or maybe you don't even know how. And honestly, I don't know which I find more pitiful." She exited the kitchen, never looking back, though she wished she had hidden cameras to see if Brooke's expression was flabbergasted.

Once she'd pulled the sheets from her bed, shoved them in the washer and remade it with a new set from her linen closet, Kaitlin felt a little guilty. She wasn't being a very good hostess. She'd taken the day off to fix up the guest room and decided to continue with her plans, even if Brooke had changed hers.

She didn't have to look in a mirror to know her own expression was stunned when she found Brooke in the guest room making up the bed. She quickly got hold of herself.

"Find everything you needed to make the bed?" Kaitlin asked in an attempt to be civil.

"Yes. I did. Everything was laid out already."

"Good. I'm going down to make more coffee after all. Want some?"

"Yes. Please."

Kaitlin almost fell to the floor in shock at hearing the word "please" come out of her stepsister's mouth. "Okay. Come on down when you're finished."

As Kaitlin scooped coffee into the basket filter, she heard Brooke's phone ring. She heard her stepsister say hello, but didn't hear any of the ensuing conversation.

Brooke entered the kitchen a few minutes later.

Attempted morning coffee with Brooke, take two.

She poured herself a cup and pointed to the extra mug she'd set out. Brooke picked it up and made herself a cup. Small victories.

"I'd like to invite you out to lunch today." Brooke

sipped her coffee, not looking at her directly. Interesting.

"That would be very nice," Kaitlin responded. Civil was the word of the day as of now.

"I'd also like for you to meet my new boyfriend for dinner. He's invited us both to dine with him tonight. I told him you have a new boyfriend. So, of course, he's invited as well."

Kaitlin lingered on the current sip of coffee, wondering if Zak would be interested in dinner. "That would be lovely. And it's very generous of you to invite Zak. I'll ask him, but I'm not certain of his plans for this evening. He might be busy."

Brooke's lips tightened, then she visibly relaxed. "Perhaps you could call him before we go out for lunch, so tonight's reservation can be adjusted either way."

Kaitlin could see Brooke was trying to make every effort and that it was costing her. "Okay. Zak works at a local garage. We can stop by there on the way out to lunch. I'd call him, but most times he can't hear his phone in the shop." She couldn't admit the truth—that she didn't actually have Zak's phone number. Perhaps she needed to change that if she could.

"Excellent." Brooke seemed to relax even more.

Kaitlin hoped Zak wouldn't be furious if she came to his work. It wasn't as though it was a dangerous place like the biker bar. What could go wrong?

CHAPTER 10

Zak had made it to work on time, but Julio had called in sick. That was troublesome for many reasons, but he did call Zak's cell to tell him the meeting with Demarco was on for early that evening. Right after he got off work from this fake job. He'd have to cut out early or find a way during the day to call Miles with the information. He might be able to access the cash if Miles had had time to set it up in a hidden location close by.

Julio hadn't sounded distressed, but rather like he had a really bad head cold. Hopefully it was a cold, and not that he'd been made as a possible informant and was tied to a chair somewhere with a broken nose being forced to lead Zak into a trap. Zak tried to shake his grim thoughts. He did have a really good imagination. Perhaps that was why he'd been able to stay alive all this time.

Midway through a busy and difficult morning, Zak was on his back under a vintage car, shoulder blades digging into concrete as he tried to reattach an obstinate starter, when someone kicked his leg. Twice. *What the fuck?*

He hated when people kicked him to get his attention while he was under a car. Why couldn't they just wait until he was finished or yell his name? He slid out from under the vehicle with a vile temper pricked and ready to start a fight, but stopped short when he sat up and saw Kaitlin standing a few feet away. She bounced nervously from one foot to the other as she waited. Trouble?

Eddie said, "Someone's here to see you. Normally I wouldn't bother you, but she's very pretty." His boss waggled his bushy eyebrows.

"Thanks," Zak managed. Kaitlin seemed very nervous. Of course, the last time she'd followed him somewhere, he'd been furious about it. Zak stood up and waved. He watched her stiffness melt from her body. She smiled and waved back.

"If you ever don't want her anymore, I'd like first dibs. She's seriously hot."

He stared right at her when he remarked, "A guy would have to be crazy or stupid to ever not want *her* anymore, and I'm not either one of those things. Go find your own girl."

Eddie laughed, his ponderous belly shaking with mirth as he lumbered away.

Zak stopped to grab a wet wipe, rubbing it over his greasy hands, wishing for the opportunity to clean up better before discovering what brought her here. Her pensive expression said she wanted to ask a favor. If it had anything to do with sex on the premises, he'd consider it. She was nothing if not sex on a stick. He'd never been so visually impacted by a woman in all his days. There was something about her feisty attitude with a hint of innocence that made his libido go pop. Every. Single. Time.

"I'm so sorry to bother you at work, Zak," she said once he got close enough. Her voice lowered to practically a whisper, when she added, "I didn't have your phone number and my stepsister invited both of us out to dinner with her new boyfriend."

"Her new boyfriend?"

"That's why she's in town, apparently. Her boyfriend is conducting business somewhere locally. She told him I live here and he wants to take us both out to dinner tonight, since you're *my* new boyfriend and all."

"It's not that I don't want to go." Zak moved closer, but didn't touch her. "But I have that rescheduled meeting to see Demarco tonight."

Her eyes widened as if she, too, suddenly remembered all that had transpired at the bar last night before rapturous sex took place. Or perhaps it was only his mind carousing in the gutter.

She said, "Right. I completely forgot."

"No problem."

Kaitlin glanced around the auto shop. "So this is where you work?"

"Yes."

She frowned. "I'm really sorry to bother you here. I just didn't know how else to get a hold of you."

"Don't worry. It's not a problem. It's still a good idea for us to pretend to be involved in public, at least for the time being. We have to keep up appearances, right?" He smiled at her, and she smiled back.

"As for my phone number, I guess I don't have yours either. But we should exchange them for our...cover, don't you think?"

"Yes. For our cover," she repeated, but with a mildly dreamy expression, which was even more dangerous.

Zak reached into his pocket for his phone. She started reciting numbers as he punched them into his contacts list.

He dialed the saved number and her phone rang in her purse. When she pushed the button to answer, he said, "Now you have my number, too."

"Thanks, Zak." She reached up, putting her palm at the V of his T-shirt where he'd unzipped his coveralls.

He wanted to kiss her, but not in this environment. Not when he had grease splattered all over him from an earlier oil change gone wrong. Not when he was undercover and living in this fake life. Not when he was pretending to be a low-life criminal trying to score illegal goods in a deal with a trafficker.

"For what?"

Kaitlin gazed into his soul by way of his eyes. "For last night and today. I really am sorry to bother you at work."

Zak noticed another figure approaching out of the corner of his eye. He glanced away from Kaitlin's hypnotic stare to see her stepsister on a fast approach.

He cleared his throat, breaking the trance and took a half step back.

"Can he make it to dinner, or not?"

"Sorry." Zak answered for himself. "I have to work late."

"How late?" Brooke asked.

Zak shrugged. "Not sure."

"Well, my boyfriend just called. He also has a meeting in the early evening and wondered if we could push our dinner to a late one."

"How late?" Zak asked.

"Will you be finished by nine?"

In fact, he likely *would* be finished by then. "Probably."

"We have reservations for four at the Prendergast." It was the very definition of fine dining in this small town. And the only such place of its class within fifty miles.

"Okay," Zak said. "Kaitlin and I will meet you there at nine."

"Excellent." Brooke turned and walked away, making another phone call as she headed to Kaitlin's car.

"Thanks, Zak." Kaitlin moved closer again, putting

her hand where it had been dislodged when he stepped away.

"It should be interesting at least. Plus, I've always wanted to eat there."

"Me, too."

"I'll pick you up half an hour before our reservation. Okay?"

She nodded, patted his chest twice with a wistful look. With luck, her look meant she wanted to strip him out of his dirty coveralls and get him a different kind of dirty as they rolled around on the floor licking and kissing each other with erotic abandon. The more likely scenario was that his libido was still carousing in the gutter.

"See you tonight." She finally walked away and Zak released a breath he hadn't realized he'd held.

Not surprisingly, the day dragged by after that. He glanced at the clock about every five minutes, thinking each time an hour must have passed. He contacted Miles on his lunch break and discovered The Organization's shortsighted attitude with regard to the new player Demarco was afraid of.

After being undercover in this role for weeks, they also wanted to change the arrest parameters. Instead of putting the money into circulation to see where it went, they wanted to bring Demarco down sooner rather than later.

They had already put the money in a place where Zak could retrieve it for the initial deal. But they were emphatic that they didn't want to postpone Demarco's takedown for a mystery guest who scared him. They decided to use it as leverage, assuming Demarco would talk once they had him in custody.

Zak didn't share that assessment and said as much to Miles. "What the hell? If this is the route we take, not only have I wasted my time playing biker dude criminal for no discernable reason, we've finally gotten some leverage with the added bonus of possibly getting someone higher up, and they want to fold the tents and leave town with only a mid-level thug and his crew?"

"There are no guarantees of that in any scenario we put forth. The Organization wants results. Immediate results. Yesterday, if you please."

"That's crazy, stupid and a fucking waste of my time. This could be very big. Honestly, I don't think you can count on Demarco being a rat. That's not who he is."

Miles countered quickly with, "Or we could lose Demarco completely because he's tired of waiting around for you to produce the money you've promised." So he had a small point.

"Just go in as planned, Zak. Wear your GPS tracker. Have your phone turned on so we can listen in. The code for go is Echo. The abort code to stop us from coming in guns a-blazing is Whiskey."

"Got it."

"But I'll warn you now; you better use the Whiskey code only as a last resort. *And* only if something goes terribly wrong. Not because you think there might be a chance that we can snag the other guy, too."

Damn. Using the abort code would keep him in this undercover role a bit longer. He wasn't anxious to leave so soon after spending time with Kaitlin. But that dream was so far down on his list of official concerns, he shouldn't even let himself think it. He shouldn't see her again regardless. He had his orders, and the mission took priority.

"You won't hear from me until after this goes down, but I'm listening. Okay?"

"Yes." Zak hung up, wondering how devastated Kaitlin was going to be if he didn't show up to take her to dinner at the swankiest place in town. If they took

Demarco down tonight, the arrests, transfers and paperwork would take a lot of time.

The longest day ever at the garage finally ended. He clocked out, threw his oil-spattered coveralls in the bin, and roared his motorcycle through town like he always did when he headed for his rental home.

As per usual, Kaitlin ruffled her curtains the moment he pulled his bike into the driveway. He casually looked over one shoulder as he dismounted with an extra twist in his hips for her benefit, and was surprised to see not Kaitlin but her stepsister staring at his ass.

He looked away, his libido deflating. He was not the least bit interested in Kaitlin's snotty, high-maintenance stepsister.

Zak hurried into his house and got ready for the meeting with Demarco. Fifteen minutes later he was back out the door. The curtains next door ruffled once more as he got on his bike, but he didn't look in case it was Brooke again. No need to fan that flame in the least.

With a GPS tracker woven into the shirt he wore and his cell phone covertly prepared to record the conversation live, he was as ready as he'd ever be. He also had backup coms if needed, but hated having something stuck in his ear for the duration, always worrying someone would notice and realize what he was really doing.

Before he left the driveway, Zak did a subtle radio check with the lead guy on the communications crew. They assured him they were standing by.

Zak planned to meet with Demarco at the Devil's Playground, give him the location of the stash of hidden marked money, follow him out there to ensure Demarco was happy, and then give the Echo code for the immediate takedown. It was still a stupid plan, but he didn't get to make the call this time.

He roared away from his rental house, figuring the

memory he'd made there with Kaitlin last night was the only one he'd get, which was a shame. But better for her in the long run.

Zak drove into the lot, parked his bike and had barely made it inside the loud bar before realizing tonight was about to be very long, and not in any way the one he'd planned.

Lunch with Brooke had gone much differently than Kaitlin had expected. Her stepsister was nice to her. Naturally, Kaitlin was wary through the entire meal, waiting for the other shoe to drop and for Brooke to start acting like she always did with brag after brag and a level of one-upmanship that only her stepsister had ever accomplished with a straight face.

But she had not dropped her nice façade once. Today's noontime meal had been like a lunch between two sisters should be. It had been filled with laughter, shared confidences, good conversation and great food. First time ever.

Brooke mentioned her new boyfriend and implied that there might be more to the relationship coming soon. She hinted that a ring might be on its way in the near future.

"How long have you been dating him?" Kaitlin asked.

"Long enough," her stepsister responded mischievously. That meant not long. Whatever.

Kaitlin came away from their lunch with the notion that perhaps Brooke's boyfriend wanted to take their relationship to a new level. Part of this trip was business, but she suspected it was also partly about meeting Brooke's family. Or perhaps to see how well they got on together while traveling.

Kaitlin genuinely wished her well. "I hope your new romance works out the way you want it to, Brooke."

"Thanks, sis." Brooke's response sounded sincere. "I'm not certain how things will turn out, but I do want to move forward with a relationship. I think the new man in my life might be *the one*."

After lunch, they returned to Kaitlin's house. Brooke spent the rest of the afternoon in her room, emerging a few hours before their reservation time to get together with her boyfriend prior to his meeting. He sent a limo for her, and said he would send it back for Kaitlin and her date to whisk them to the restaurant.

Kaitlin had tried to decline, but Brooke insisted. She hoped Zak was okay with it, not wanting to call and ask him because she figured he was already at the bar with Mr. Demarco.

She didn't know exactly where their relationship was going. She certainly didn't want to know if he was part of anything illegal. Mr. Demarco was probably involved in any number of underhanded dealings, but she hoped with foolish desire that Zak wasn't truly the criminal bad boy he seemed.

It was a future conversation she didn't look forward to. She'd only wanted him to perform one task. And he had, brilliantly. Now she wanted more, but not if it meant being part of any illegal dealings. That was a deal breaker as far as she was concerned. She put that discussion aside for now. After tonight's dinner was soon enough for serious talks about their relationship. If they even had one.

Kaitlin waited patiently for Zak to arrive for their double date. She'd changed three times before finding something she liked. It was too late to change again. The restaurant was pretty upscale so she'd settled on a suitably expensive dress, another one of the castoffs her stepsister had given her.

There were perks to being the same size. She got all of Brooke's expensive, fashionable hand-me-downs. The difference was Kaitlin appreciated it, whereas her sister would never wear a used garment.

After today's singular, stress-free lunch, Kaitlin was heartened that her sister seemed to have changed. She was acting differently, maybe thanks to this new relationship of hers. Kaitlin was only worried that Brooke hadn't known this man in her life for very long, but didn't want to rain on her stepsister's parade or sour her pleasing attitude.

Was Kaitlin wrong about both her stepsister and her own new "boyfriend" and heading for heartache on two fronts? She soon put both difficult topics out of her head and waited by the window she usually used to watch for Zak and his amazing butt.

Unfortunately, she couldn't see the clock from where she sat. Calculating the time it would take to get to the restaurant kept her fidgeting down, but didn't get rid of it completely.

When the time she expected him had come and gone by ten minutes, Kaitlin wondered if she was about to be stood up. The new calculation became, how long should she wait before taking the limo alone when it arrived and admitting to her stepsister she'd been stood up?

CHAPTER 11

Across the room of the Devil's Playground, an unexpected someone was playing pool and sipping beers with Diego Demarco. Zak looked away to cover his stunned reaction, as if suddenly intrigued by the raggedy leather barstools and equally beat up counter just inside the door. There were others in Demarco's crew sprinkled around the room, but Zak didn't take note. His concentration was squarely on the newcomer, even as he avoided eye contact.

"Zak, come meet my new friend," Demarco called out. Zak forced a blasé expression, turned and put one foot in front of the other until he reached them.

Demarco's reptilian smile sent a red glaring flag up Zak's spine, but not as much as seeing Miles Turner, dressed down wearing jeans and a leather jacket, in the role of Demarco's new "friend." What in the fuckety fuck was going on here tonight?

"What if I'm not in the mood to make a new friend?" Zak searched Miles's face for clues as to what the fuck he was doing here.

"Come on, friend. My name is Miles. Let's share a whiskey and get to know each other," Miles—*his secret undercover handler*—said.

Zak turned to Demarco. "I do not want a whiskey or a new friend. I work alone. You know that." So now they'd both used the Whiskey code to abort.

"Touché," Demarco said with a laugh. "You're right. Truth is, he's more of a competitor than a comrade. You have quite a gut instinct for such things."

"What's going on, Diego? Who the fuck is this? Why the fuck should I make his acquaintance?"

Demarco bent to make a shot in the corner pocket before he answered. "There has been a little change in our initial plan. This man," he pointed to Miles, "is someone who comes highly recommended by another well-trusted compatriot of mine. He's offering a similar deal to yours. I am put in the difficult position of having to choose where to put my narrow business interests. I can sell my product to you. Or I can give this new man, who is favored by someone I already trust, my business. Or you can relax your rules on working alone and compete."

"Why does there need to be competition?"

Demarco looked thoughtful for a moment. "As you know, I've had traitorous activities persist in the western region of my business. They *have* been resolved, but I continue to look for more, just in case. My compatriot has informed me of a rat in my organization. This possible deal with Miles is like compensation and gratitude for that timely information."

"Okay. That's reasonable," Zak said, not liking where this conversation was going.

"Yes. Well, I am considering a new business partner for that area to help control that aspect of my business. I need people I can trust to run things in remote locations."

"Who is this compatriot of yours?"

"An old friend from long ago, someone I trusted. We've renewed our friendship and other unrelated commerce dealings. In fact, he came into town early to catch up on old times before getting down to business. You may have noticed him last night as you were leaving. The well-guarded gentleman?"

"Not to cut you short, but I don't see how this involves me or a possible competitor for the same business." Zak sent a purposeful gaze over to Miles, along with a healthy *what the fuck* stare added in.

"Cheeky bastard," Miles said with a laugh, taking a swig of his beer and giving Zak a look that suggested he should change his attitude.

Demarco smiled, but Zak could tell it was barely tolerant. Clearly, he didn't like Zak's refusal to fall in with his plans.

"Do you have the money this time?" Demarco asked.

"Yes. I always had the money. I just don't carry it on me."

Demarco made a face, as if uncertain of his facts. "Are you certain you have the correct funds available to me?"

"Yes. My funds are solid. What do you know that I don't, Diego?"

"With regard to my business being infiltrated by traitors, the troubling news given to me by my old friend involves someone you know. In fact, it was the man who introduced us."

"Oh?" Fuck. Julio. Now what?

"I need to know, my friend, was Julio helping you gather the funds?"

"Julio?" he managed, but the spit in his mouth had dried up like he'd just swallowed half a desert's worth of sand. Fuckety fuck. This was very bad.

Miles scratched his face twice with two fingers before hooking them around the mouth of his bottle of beer, giving Zak the silent signal they'd established long ago. It meant that everything up was now down. Or rather, *it's opposite day, so act accordingly.*

Zak immediately said, "No. Julio hasn't been helping me at all. The truth is, I was going to talk to you about him last night before I was rushed out. He's been acting very strange. I don't know if we should trust him."

Demarco, who'd been walking around to the other side of the pool table for a better shot, stopped mid-stride and stared at Zak like he'd grown a third eye. "Is that so?"

"Yep. In fact, he wasn't at the garage today. And it isn't the first time that's happened either. I don't know what he's up to, good or bad, but I wanted to ensure you understood that it's got nothing to do with me. We just work at the same place. He told me about you and set up our first meeting, but that's it. I work alone for a reason. I don't trust easily."

Zak casually scratched behind his ear, at the same time pushing the button that activated his ear bud. Another member of Miles's crew was already speaking. The message whispering in his head repeated over and over.

—owledge. Julio is dead. His body was found with our marked money in the gas station bathroom. The new stash is in the backyard shed of your next-door neighbor to the north. Shit. Kaitlin's house. *Acknowledge.* Then it repeated that Julio was dead and so on. Zak turned the receiver off and stared at Miles. Catching his gaze, he brushed his left index finger down his right eye, meaning he understood the message.

Miles seemed to relax a bit. "So, are you ready to do this deal? Where's your money, hotshot?"

"None of your business. I don't know you. Friend of a friend or not, I don't trust you yet."

Miles laughed, but underlying his amusement was relief. He'd obviously inserted himself into this mess as the only way of keeping Zak from telling Demarco to pick up the payment at a place where he knew a traitor had been caught. He'd have to process Julio being dead later. Miles's presence was dangerous as hell. But Zak was more than a little grateful. Miles had once again proved himself an excellent handler in the risky business they both worked in.

Demarco said, "This man comes recommended by someone I trust. He was vetted long ago. Given my level of suspicion of late, you know that is saying quite a lot."

Zak shrugged. "Fine, he's been vetted. That doesn't mean he's the best man for this job or someone I need to know."

"I'm proposing that the two of you do this deal together."

"What the fuck?" Zak wasn't truly opposed to working with Miles, but he had to pretend to be hostile at first. Demarco had to believe he'd talked Zak into it. It would be far more suspicious if he just agreed to this new change right out of the gate. "As I said, I prefer to work alone."

Miles raised his arms. "Just hear me out, hotshot. We can put our money together and make this initial deal double the size. We split the costs *and* the profits, but Diego makes a bigger sale at the outset. Trust me. It's a win for all of us."

Somehow, Zak didn't feel like any of this would end up being a triumph. He remained silent, calculating how long to dispute the change before coming around.

"Where is the lovely Kaitlin tonight, Zak?" Demarco asked abruptly.

Zak frowned, mentally preparing himself for the battle to come. Demarco's stance became belligerent. "Isn't that your woman's name?" Without waiting for an answer, he persisted, "Did you satisfy her before you came here tonight? You know how demanding she can be, right?" He laughed at his own stupid joke. The sycophants around him smiled and nodded like he'd told a real zinger.

Caught off guard by the inappropriate question, Zak answered without thinking it through. "What the fuck is it to you?" *Fuck.* The second the words crossed his lips, regret filled him.

What was wrong with him? He was supposed to be respectful to Demarco—to a point—not hostile. Arrogant, power-hungry people didn't respond well to aggression.

Demarco ignored his slip and grinned evilly. "I was wondering if she might show up again, although given your attitude, perhaps it was *you* who went unsatisfied this time," he added, chuckling like he referenced an inside joke they shared. He didn't.

Cold rage consumed Zak. He stilled, readying himself to strike Demarco hard for his offensive insinuation.

Miles looked like he'd swallowed his tongue for a moment. Then he verbally stepped into the suddenly arctic blast of air between the two men. "You have a woman, Zak? Is she hot? Is she a blonde? I like blondes."

What was Miles blathering about?

Zak came back to reality. This was all for show. Demarco shouldn't be able to play his emotions in such a personal way. His fury receded. Relaxing his shoulders and forcing his body to also unwind, Zak replied, "Of course she's hot. She's *my* woman."

Demarco nodded. "I can confirm. Zak's woman is quite beautiful, in a prim, proper, virginal sort of way. Is that why you are so attached to her? Was she a virgin when you took her the first time, Zak?" A maniacal stare filled with inappropriate sexual hunger accompanied his query. Zak had calmed considerably. While his ire was up, he made every effort to keep it under control. Demarco was being a deliberate prick, trying to instigate a fight. And what was with the taunt about Kaitlin being a virgin? It wasn't like she was a teenager. Demarco was fucked up.

Zak refused to play.

"What do *you* think, Diego?" he asked, keeping a lid on his volatile emotions.

"I think it's convenient that *your woman* lives next door to you. Is that how you chose her? She was in close proximity?"

Zak forced a laugh. "That's exactly right. She's less than a minute away whenever I want her. Perhaps I should call her my *convenient* woman from now on. Just don't make any mistake about the part where she's *mine* regardless of her location." He stopped laughing, giving Demarco a threatening death stare.

Miles walked toward them, inserting himself between a furious Zak and a maniacal Demarco. "Enough talk about bitches. Let's hammer out this deal, yeah?"

Diego turned his attention to Miles and his antagonism bled away in the relaxing of his body language. Zak wasn't as quick to forgive.

Prompting the question, was Zak really about to ruin this whole undercover operation because Demarco was being a perverted prick with regard to a woman Zak had no business being involved with in the first damn place?

The doorbell rang half an hour before nine, breaking into Kaitlin's growing despair that Zak wouldn't show up. Or that he was a hardened criminal and, additionally, that her sister was just setting her up for an even crueler trick at dinner tonight, which she would have to face alone.

She shook off her foolish fears and headed for the door. Maybe she'd win points since she was ready to go and he wouldn't have to wait. They had plenty of time if

Zak wanted to, say, kiss her lipstick off. She'd have time to repair the damage. A smile shaped her mouth at the thought as she popped the door open.

He hadn't stood her up. Gratitude filled her completely.

"Wow. You look great," Zak said, his eyes widening in appreciation. His gaze slid up and down her body a couple of times before settling on her face.

Zak wore a suit with a tie. He'd shaved, and he'd even trimmed his shaggy hair, slicking it neatly back. He looked like a power broker ready for a nine-to-five workweek and poised to take over the world. "You look really different," she said, trying not to sound shocked.

He grinned. "Do I?" He rubbed one hand across his cleanly shaven jaw. He shrugged. "It feels good to clean up on occasion. You aren't disappointed, are you?"

"No! Not disappointed." *Maybe a little.* But only because now every single female they met tonight would hunger after him, not just the ones seeking a bad boy to fulfill their darker fantasies. Then again, he'd likely turn women's heads wherever he went, regardless of whether he'd shaved.

Zak hooked a thumb over his shoulder, pointing at the front of her house. "Is that limo for us?"

She peeked out her door and saw the same stretch limo that had whisked Brooke away earlier waiting for them. "Yes. Brooke's boyfriend insisted. I hope you don't mind."

"Nope." He gestured to her dress. "I don't imagine that dress would be easy to wear if we rode my motorcycle to dinner."

Kaitlin glanced over at where his bike was parked in its usual spot, wondering how she'd failed to hear him come home. He must have arrived when Brooke was still blasting music from her phone through a portable speaker.

She looked down at the shimmery sequins attached to her expensive hand-me-down, and paled at the thought of arriving at the exclusive Prendergast restaurant valet parking station straddled behind Zak on his Harley with her dress hiked up to her business for the ride over.

"It's doable, but no, not easy." She gestured for him to come in.

Gaze still over one shoulder at the limo, Zak stepped over the threshold, but not far enough to shut the front door. "Are you ready to go?"

"Yes and no."

His gaze shifted to her, right where she wanted it. A grin surfaced. "Well, which is it?"

"Yes, I'm ready to go, but if you kiss me like I want you to, then I'll have to fix my lipstick before we leave. So will you?"

"Will I?" he asked, his brows furrowing.

Kaitlin licked the center of her upper lip. "Will you ruin my lipstick before we go?" She stepped into his personal space, one hand resting on the front door's brass knob, the other snaking around his neck. She pushed her body into his. "You know what to do, right?"

"I have an idea," he said against her lips. "But be forewarned, I'm a bad boy. You should always plan on getting more than you bargained for." She drew back, winked at him as seductively as she could, and licked the entire length of her bottom lip this time in invitation. He seized her offer, and her, in a fevered and very passionate kiss.

Excellent, her libido whispered. She let go of the doorknob.

His arms tightened around her torso, crushing her deliciously into his chest as his mouth twisted against her lips, licking his way through to plunder her thoroughly. He not only ruined her lipstick, he overwhelmed her. The smooth feel of his face was different, but the intensity of the kiss hadn't wavered. Through the haze of the volcanic kiss, she heard the door close rather forcefully. He must have kicked it shut. Perfect.

Before she knew it, she was flat on her back on her own formal dining table. She was grateful she'd moved the floral centerpiece earlier, but nothing would have prompted her to stop what Zak was doing. Zak's body covered hers completely and she liked this aggressive show of dominance.

His hand bunched the fabric of her dress against her thigh. She wasn't certain what he was doing until his fingers scorched the bare skin of her inner thigh on a path straight between her legs. Just as one long finger edged beneath her panties, she managed to break the kiss and ask through her panting breaths, "What are you doing?"

He rose up slowly, a satisfied grin shaping his lipstick-stained mouth. "Thought I'd put some color in your cheeks before dinner. We have a little time before we have to leave. What do you say?"

Kaitlin weighed her options. Have sex with Zak and be a little late for dinner with her stepsister. Or forgo sex with Zak and…that was just stupid. She'd never consciously sacrifice any possible sex with Zak. Ever.

"I say yes!"

He didn't speak. His gaze remained on her face—the hint of a seductive half-smile lifting one corner of his mouth, like he knew she'd agree—as his finger continued its naughty journey into her panties. He stroked her once, twice, three times, hitting her hot spot each and every time. Her pleasure spiked. Zak leaned down, resuming the carnal kiss as he fingered her with expert precision.

Kaitlin was seconds away from another epic climax when her phone started ringing across the room. The interruption didn't change Zak's determination one single bit. He continued kissing her and stoking her like there wasn't a limo waiting outside, like her phone wasn't ringing a warning to check the time.

If anything, Zak sped his strokes. An orgasm she didn't expect pre-dinner rose within her like a pervasive sensual fog ready to take over the night. She broke the kiss, sucked in a deep breath, spiraling out of control as she came in a hard, gratifying rush.

She screamed Zak's name to the ceiling of her dining room more than once as wave after wave of wave of riotous pleasure filled her body and soul. He pressed his face into her neck, nibbling her sensitive skin as she finished writhing in utter madness from her recent climax.

Zak lifted up and pulled his hand from between her legs. Completely boneless, her body flattened against the rumpled tablecloth, arms wide and legs dangling. "Want me to get your phone?" he asked in a low, amused tone.

"I don't care," she said truthfully, speaking from her very satisfied soul.

He chuckled. "Think it's your sister checking up on us?"

"I don't care," she repeated to his further amusement. He slipped an arm beneath her back, lifting her from the table. The tablecloth was not only wrinkled from the erotic foray, but askew and about to slither to the floor.

She didn't care about that either. She felt too good to do much more than attempt to make her legs work so she could stand up.

Zak helped steady her as she leaned heavily into the table's edge. "You were absolutely right," he remarked with amusement. "Your lipstick is totally messed up after kissing me."

"I see that." She brushed a fingertip over his lower lip. "You're wearing half of it, too."

He shrugged and tightened his hand around her upper arm, getting very serious. "One thing I need to know for future reference," he paused, staring deeply into her eyes, "was *that* the way you wanted to be kissed?"

"Absolutely. Yes."

His grin surfaced again. "Good. I'll note that and tuck it away. Are you ready to go fix your lipstick? Because the limo is waiting, you know. We don't want to be *too* late for dinner. We'd have to explain." He winked conspiratorially, wearing her lipstick all around his mouth. "And I would."

"Explain?"

"I'd be willing to tell your stepsister exactly why we are late tonight. That's what bad boys do."

He pointed her toward the half-bath in the hallway, and then helped her walk a few steps in that direction. "Okay. I'm going. No need for explanations." It took her a minute to get herself under control once she stepped into the small bathroom. Holy wow, he was so intoxicating.

She revived a bit upon seeing her rose-colored, lipstick-smeared mouth. She looked like the worst of all the bad girls she'd ever known. A thrill rode down her spine as she fixed her lipstick, wiping off the old and applying the new coat, noting Zak was also right about the heightened color in her cheeks.

Sixty seconds later she exited the small room, grabbed her purse and phone as Zak opened the front door. He closed it behind him. She locked it, and together they strolled down the walkway to the street. He'd wiped her telltale lipstick from his face, too.

The driver waited by the rear door of the limo, opening it for them as they approached. Once they were both settled inside, the door closed and they were alone for a moment.

"By the way," Zak said in a low voice. "I love

hearing you scream my name over and over when I bury my hand between your legs to make you come. Next time, though, I want to do it with my tongue. Okay?"

Kaitlin's cheeks heated, but the driver got into the front of the vehicle before she could respond. Zak looked very satisfied that he'd put her off guard momentarily.

"We'll be there in no time, folks," the driver said politely, pulling away from her house.

"Can't wait," Zak said.

"Are you going to behave this evening?" she asked.

He shrugged. "It's possible." She relaxed into the back of the leather seat. "But I wouldn't count on it," he added, turning toward her in his seat and brushing a finger possessively across the center of one breast.

CHAPTER 12

Zak usually wasn't someone who enjoyed public attention when seducing his woman, but he was also playing a part.

While he was mostly Zak Langston, undercover agent, trying to bring down a nasty local cartel, he was also playing the part of Zak Thornton, a biker bad boy with a reputation to uphold and a brand new woman in his life.

Kaitlin moved his hand from her breast gently, stroking him with her fingertips and placing it palm down on her thigh. The smile on her lips said she wasn't angry, she just didn't want a public display. She had a point. The limo driver didn't need to run off the road watching them put on a sex show in the backseat, but then again, Zak wouldn't turn her down if *she* suggested it.

He was amazed he'd been able to act as cool and collected as he had after arriving at Kaitlin's for the auspicious dinner out. He'd gone from expecting he would have to ditch her forever after arresting Demarco, to hurriedly cleaning up, shaving and cutting his hair to make it to this posh dinner on time.

Down was up and up was down.

Miles and Demarco had set up yet another meet tomorrow evening to bring in the trusted compatriot and finalize the joint deal.

In this secretive, often dangerous job, Zak always tried to be prepared for things to change. Scenarios like this were typically fluid and always altered to some degree regardless of meticulous planning. He wished he'd had a chance to have a short conversation with Miles regarding not only his insertion into this undercover operation, but also how he was involved with Demarco's friend. Hopefully they'd chat later tonight. Or at least before tomorrow evening's big double buyer deal extravaganza.

Zak had a bad feeling when he heard Julio had called in sick, despite the personal phone call from the man himself. It hadn't gotten better when he'd arrived at the Devil's Playground and seen Miles instead of Julio. Until he'd heard what had really happened through the ear bud, Zak had expected Julio to show up at the bar.

The last time he'd seen Julio was the night Kaitlin changed the course of his evening. Julio left the Devil's Playground soon after she arrived, presumably on an errand for Demarco. He'd been directly behind Zak when Kaitlin came in. Zak hadn't even seen him leave, but he'd had his hands and mind full of his new woman. Julio hadn't come back by the time Zak was hustled out with Kaitlin. Or Zak hadn't seen him, anyway.

Even with Miles inserted to help, Julio's death put Zak's relationship with Demarco in a precarious position.

"Did your, um, meeting go okay?" Kaitlin asked shyly.

Zak wasn't certain he should even speak generally about the disastrous gathering. He decided to be elusive with any information from that arena. He was very good at being vague. "Not sure yet. We'll have to see."

Demarco was still a power hungry carnivore in this nasty business. Zak's job here wasn't over yet, which was both good news and bad news, the good news being he could spend more time with Kaitlin, the bad news was she still had to be involved on the periphery of these dealings.

It was clear Demarco wouldn't let her fade back from the business. He'd even asked after her as Zak left the bar. He'd had to clamp down on his urge to punch the man's sparkling white teeth down his throat for even saying her name.

Miles had again stepped in to calm things down in more ways than one, enabling Zak to come to this dinner and offer not only his company for a date, but his protection moving forward. He'd have to guard her safety more than ever.

Kaitlin didn't question his vague answers. She simply nodded and changed the subject to a lighter topic. "I had an interesting lunch with my stepsister earlier. She was nice to me."

"Is that unusual?" Zak didn't have any sisters, only lots and lots of brothers. Whereas boys physically beat on each other to communicate, he suspected sisters used their words instead. That said, he'd witnessed a couple of hair-pulling, fist-to-the-face girl fights that would make any self-respecting bad boy cringe in fear.

"It was a bit like being in the middle of a 'What Would You Do?' episode."

"Why's that?"

"She's never nice to me. Ever. But today was like, what would you do if your typically mean-girl sister suddenly treated you like an actual person? I kept waiting for her to turn into the bitchy, know-it-all braggart I know she's so good at being, but that side of her personality never came out. I'm not certain what to expect tonight, but I want you to be prepared for either eventuality."

"Well, whatever happens, I've got your back. If she's bitchy, braggy or mean, we can always get up and leave."

"I don't know that I'd have the balls to do that."

Zak grinned. "I do. In fact, I have enough for both of us."

"No argument there. So maybe we should have a signal."

"Such as?" Zak was already juggling quite a few signals with regard to his earlier meeting. He didn't need more to memorize for this coming dinner.

"Like I could tug my ear and that means, let's make our excuses and go. Or I could put my hand on your thigh under the table if we need to stay."

He gave her his best bad boy grin and said, "For the record, all I can think about right now is having your hand on my thigh throughout dinner, regardless of your meaning."

"Very funny. Is sex always on your mind?"

"Yes. I'm a bad boy. In fact, it's the *only* thing on my mind. Didn't you get that memo?"

Without skipping a beat, Kaitlin said, "Nope. At the good girl academy, we were never allowed to read any bad boy memos."

Zak laughed out loud. "Good one." She settled back against the leather seat, her rapturous gaze putting even worse bad boy thoughts into his head.

He grabbed her fingers, pressed a chaste kiss to her knuckles, but then turned her hand over and licked her wrist with the tip of his tongue. He'd truly love to lick his way between her thighs right now. Did they have time?

Kaitlin's mouth fell open a bit. Whether it was in

surprise, a sudden spike of desire, or that she'd read his mind regarding the possible time available for licking her body elsewhere while they were seated right here in the limo, he didn't know.

He did know he wanted her. Maybe the driver wouldn't notice if they managed a discreet quickie in the back seat. The lighting was low.

But in the next second, the vehicle slowed and made a turn before coming to a complete stop. The driver put the vehicle in park and announced, "Here we are. I'll be around to open your door." He hopped out, leaving them alone.

Zak leaned in to kiss her mouth, but she turned her cheek at the last second. "Don't ruin my lipstick just yet, okay? Let's save it for during dinner in case my sister acts up." She flashed a quick grin, and he knew there wasn't anything he wouldn't do for her in this moment.

Resisting the urge to lick her face, just to see how she'd react, Zak chuckled. "All right, I'll behave for now. No promises on how long I'll last though. Bad boys have short attention spans."

She patted his knee twice and turned as the door whipped open in front of a valet parking zone. They were also right next to the elaborately fancy doors to the restaurant. Having her hand on his leg put dangerous thoughts in his head. He needed to settle down.

Regardless of his teasing, Zak truly didn't plan to be a douche bag at dinner. He'd fit in. He'd make nice. He'd continue the charade that they were a romantic couple because he had to.

A restaurant employee smiled and opened the front door, welcoming them to the Prendergast. They stepped into a lush foyer. Just ahead was the elaborately carved wooden maître d' stand. Zak put a hand low on her back and they approached it. He could see several tables through the arched entry into the restaurant. The place looked crowded, opulent and filled with those in the wealthiest class.

Perhaps he could make Brooke believe he was serious about Kaitlin. She could leave town in a day or two convinced Kaitlin was involved with a bad boy and tell whatever tales she wanted. That seemed to be Kaitlin's goal.

Whatever else their relationship entailed, he did want to be the guy Kaitlin needed in her life right now. But would she be angry to discover his real line of work wasn't so much bad boy as privately hired undercover agent? Too soon to tell.

If she expected him to walk her down a petal-strewn aisle anytime soon, she'd be disappointed. He'd seen other agents maintain a family life completely separate from this underbelly world of criminal activity, but that existence wasn't without sacrifices. He didn't think he could do it.

There were personal costs to his chosen career that Zak had never considered until this moment. He glanced at Kaitlin and was rewarded with her grateful grin. She was happy, exuberantly so. Honestly, Zak was proud of himself for putting the rosy color in her cheeks, remembering with very male satisfaction how she screamed his name repeatedly as she'd climaxed.

A burly guy bustled past him and stopped at the edge of the restaurant's main entry, hovering between the bar and the front door. He looked familiar. Was it the other guard with Demarco's mystery man? Quite possibly.

As they waited to be shown to their table, Zak reflected briefly on the meeting with Demarco earlier. The memory of entering the Devil's Playground for the rescheduled meeting made his *oh-fuck-o-meter* spike even now.

With Miles and a completely unknown entity involved in the deal, Zak was off the rails, in new territory and making things up as he went along. The most troubling news from his point of view was where they'd hidden the second stash of money.

He hadn't wanted to rifle through Kaitlin's shed, since he knew she was home. Besides, he didn't have time. If Demarco had known the new money location, there would have been another litany of humorless jokes regarding the problems of having a woman in such close proximity and how it made deals of this nature tricky.

Miles suggested they converge tomorrow night with their respective financial stashes at an abandoned warehouse on the opposite end of town from the bar and make arrangements for the transfer of the product.

Tomorrow was going to be the *big* day. Tonight would probably be his last with Kaitlin. He should take advantage of it. Miles could suck it if he disagreed. Zak also needed to find out what Miles had in mind for tomorrow's meeting. He'd have to contact him later on using his hidden phone. Yet another conversation he didn't look forward to.

Zak was juggling so many balls it was a wonder they weren't pelting him in the head every time he stood still for longer than a minute.

His reverie broke when the chilly maître d' in this very swanky restaurant came back to his podium, ready to show them to their table, mentioning in a snotty tone that their dinner guests were already seated. They were less than ten minutes late. The maître d' could suck it, too.

Zak wanted to mention that they'd been standing around his podium for quite a while, but swallowed his sarcasm, took Kaitlin's arm and guided her past table after table of chicly dressed, attractive rich people. Out of the corner of his eye, Zak noticed the second bodyguard seated just inside the small hallway leading to the restrooms. He averted his head to keep from being recognized. That meant Demarco's friend was definitely somewhere in the restaurant. Great. This was about to be the longest fucking dinner ever.

Their guide stopped at a horseshoe-shaped booth where two people were already seated. The empty far side of the half circle table waited for them. Brooke was seated in the center.

Kaitlin slid into the booth and scooted next to her stepsister, leaving Zak's seat directly across from none other than the mystery man who'd frightened Demarco at last night's failed meeting. The man stood, offering his hand. "Hello. I'm Ernesto Montego. Delighted to meet you."

"Zak Thornton." He shook the other man's hand firmly then sat across from him. "Thanks for the dinner invitation," he managed to say lightly, even though his *o-fuck-o-meter* was pinging wildly.

Montego was the trusted compatriot Miles had been vetted through. Had Miles known Zak was having dinner with him tonight?

If he didn't, the better question had to do with Miles's reaction when he found out.

Tonight's conversation would have to be carefully controlled, adding more than a few razor-sharp knives to the objects Zak was trying to juggle above his head.

CHAPTER 13

Kaitlin sensed rather than knew for a fact that Zak was agitated. Perhaps things hadn't gone well at his meeting with the beautiful demon she'd met the night before.

She smiled at Brooke as her stepsister's boyfriend rose to shake hands with Zak.

"Hello. I'm Ernesto Montego. Delighted to meet you."

Zak shook the man's well-manicured hand. "Zak Thornton. Thanks for the dinner invitation."

"It's my pleasure." Ernesto gestured for Zak to sit as Brooke spoke up. "Ernesto, this is my sister, Kaitlin Price. Kaitlin, meet Ernesto."

He nodded as Kaitlin said, "Pleased to meet you, Mr. Montego."

"Call me Ernesto, please," he said jovially. "Your sister is very important to me. I hope we can be friends."

"Of course."

Ernesto then started talking, seemingly endlessly, about how he'd met Brooke, how he'd wooed her and how he wanted to make her part of his permanent romantic life. Unfortunately, he came across as the very definition of pompous and arrogant only ten words into his long speech, which was mostly all about him.

It was in this moment that Kaitlin wondered what in the ever-loving hell she'd gotten herself into.

She barely got along with her stepsister on a good day. Beside her, Zak was a veritable stranger about whom she knew almost nothing beyond a few carnal, erotic, delicious things. He had a great ass, his kisses were awe-inspiring, and he could make her scream epically—on a dining room table, no less—without even taking her clothes off. While that was all good in its own right, it was not polite dinner conversation.

Since she wasn't planning to talk about sex, how would they fill the evening's conversation? What did any of them have in common? Maybe it wouldn't be an issue, since Ernesto didn't seem like he was ever going to stop talking or patting himself on the back for being a perfect man of the world. She glanced at Zak, but he didn't seem bothered. Perhaps she was the only one with misgivings.

Why in the world had she agreed to this foolish dinner charade?

"How long have the two of you been together?" Ernesto asked all of a sudden, opening yet another vast crater of awkward conversation with the seemingly innocuous ice-breaker question.

Kaitlin inhaled deeply and slapped a smile in place. Perhaps it was time to tug on her ear already and leave.

Zak spoke before she could try out the signal. "Not long. But we live next door to each other. We see each other quite a bit." In addition to saying the exact correct thing, he also looked deeply into her eyes as if she were the only person in the room. When he gently lifted her hand to his lips and kissed her knuckles, she momentarily forgot anyone else was even at the table.

"Convenient." Ernesto's nod was on the condescending side, as if he found the idea of the two of them dating to be a spectacle worthy of a zoo. His smarmy tone brought her out of her happy dream world.

Was he being a shit? Did he think they were faking?

"It is," Zak said. "Plus, Kaitlin is quite special." He put his arm around her possessively, squeezing her shoulder with his strong fingers. She leaned in his direction. If the night was going to hell, at least she was sharing it with the hottest guy in the room.

"Clearly," Ernesto said, but his tone had turned disapproving. Was she being paranoid? How had he rushed to that judgment so quickly? Where was a member of the restaurant staff to distract them from this uncomfortable line of questioning?

A waiter appeared as if magically answering Kaitlin's internal plea for rescue to take their drink orders. As it turned out, she had nothing to worry about with regard to awkward conversation. Ernesto resumed talking as the waiter stood there, about himself, of course. All the while, Zak either gently rubbed her shoulder or lightly rasped his fingernails on her bare back as if he didn't want to stop touching her. She liked it very much.

"I don't know if Brooke told you," Ernesto said as if sharing a secret. "But I'm renowned for my knowledge in the world of gourmet food, and I'm quite the wine connoisseur." Brooke fawned like he was a demi-god. Kaitlin put on a show of being impressed and made all the appropriate noises of amazement, but she wasn't.

"Will you allow me to select our adult beverages this evening?" he asked as if he'd just told the best joke ever.

Adult beverages? Really? She wanted to roll her eyes, but resisted the urge.

She looked at Zak. He looked back with a loving smile, shrugged and deferred to her.

"Please do," she responded for both of them.

Ernesto ordered a bottle of something foreign she guessed was from either Italy or Spain or possibly Portugal. She couldn't tell which language he spoke, but the waiter seemed to understand and scurried off to do Mr. Arrogant's bidding.

All the while Zak put his focus solely on her as if Ernesto didn't bother him in the least. She should take a page out of his book and relax. And she tried, she truly did.

However, after only a few more minutes in Ernesto's company, Kaitlin was even less impressed with her stepsister's new boyfriend. He was the very definition of pompous, condescending and all things she hated about people who liked to lord over the fact that they had money and spent it on expensive, civilized things, not like the peons of the world scratching out a living, wasting their money on what he considered crap.

Ernesto acted like he'd done them a favor by bringing them to dinner and showing them what the *good life* truly consisted of. That was all the encouragement Brooke needed. She was back in her element.

She went the mean girl route for dinner, proving she really couldn't be nice two meals in a row. When she wasn't making mean comments, she fed into Ernesto's self-important attitude. They were two of a kind. The obvious act her stepsister put on at lunch was in no way translated to the late dinner meal.

Kaitlin couldn't help but feel a little betrayed. Perhaps gullible was a better word. She should have known her stepsister hadn't changed a single bit.

Zak nodded and made the appropriate noises when Ernesto was looking for praise, but mostly he touched Kaitlin, smiled at her and made her feel like the belle of the ball. She fell a little more in love with him with each passing moment in their disagreeable dinner companions' company.

Once the wine arrived at the table, Ernesto made a big deal of showing off his prowess by repeatedly sniffing the cork and then sampling a small taster glass of wine not once or twice but three times before allowing the waiter to pour wine for the rest of them.

Twenty minutes after the wine came to the table, Kaitlin took a sip of the vilest tasting liquid she'd ever put in her mouth. She wished she could spit it out, but managed to swallow, smile and promptly lie convincingly that it was great.

Ernesto shrugged as if it was a foregone conclusion that he'd selected the perfect *adult beverage* for the meal. Kaitlin went back to pondering her estimate of how long a night it was going to be.

The waiter returned to take their dinner orders. Kaitlin was poised to order the restaurant's lauded signature chicken dish with a caper and pine nut sauce, but Ernesto had different plans.

"I hope you'll allow me to order dinner for all of you." He didn't wait for an answer.

Turning to the waiter, he announced, "We'd all like the filet mignon." He *did* select the most expensive meal on the menu, but it wasn't what Kaitlin wanted. A heavy steak dinner so late would make her lethargic until tomorrow.

"Very good, sir." The waiter asked Brooke, "How would you like your steak prepared, ma'am?"

Ernesto said angrily, "Well done, naturally! For all four meals." The waiter paled as Ernesto blustered on about not wanting a single drop of blood on their plates or any pink meat, stating he planned to inspect each steak when it arrived at their table for the proper brown internal color.

Kaitlin exchanged a look with Zak that she couldn't read, expecting him to change his order, but he shrugged and deferred to Ernesto. She liked her steak a nice medium, but resigned herself to an expensive dry meat puck, silently thanking Zak for going along and not making a scene.

Given that she didn't know much about Zak or what he was capable of beyond his protective tendencies or his prowess in the bedroom, Kaitlin fell more in love with him as the evening progressed and he went along with the ever-present haughty madness, always keeping his primary focus on her.

She did make a special personal note of when Zak took one sip of the wine and then never touched his glass again.

True to his word, Ernesto inspected each of their steaks by cutting them in half to ensure no pink—or juiciness—had survived. It hadn't.

Zak ate most of his meat. Kaitlin pushed hers around on the plate and hid most of it beneath the garnish. Perhaps the chef had provided the large kale leaf for just that purpose.

"So did you attend any college, Zak? I mean, didn't you ever want to become more than a mere mechanic?" Ernesto asked as a lavish strawberry studded cheesecake was served for dessert. At least he couldn't screw up this part of the meal.

"Nah, I was never much into higher learning," Zak said, seemingly unfazed by Ernesto's insinuation that he was a *mere* anything. "But I'm good with my hands, and I like working on cars." He stared right into her eyes when he mentioned being *good* with his hands. While she could attest to that personally, she didn't.

"So no education at all then." Ernesto shook his head like he was disappointed in Zak's lack of ambition.

"I went to a specialized school and got a certificate to work on engines. That's it." He took a bite of the cheesecake, his eyes closing seemingly in appreciation of the flavorful dessert.

Ernesto gave him a tolerant look, as if unsurprised that Zak didn't have any loftier educational goals. He turned to Kaitlin. "Now *you* have a degree in

FIONA ROARKE

business or accounting or the like, is that correct, Kaitlin?"

She swallowed the mouthful of creamy strawberry dessert that congealed in her mouth the moment he turned his attention on her. "Yes. I have a degree in accounting."

Brooke took the occasion to slap her down. "Daddy tried to get her to take the exam for her CPA credentials, to no avail." Her stepsister rolled her eyes as if Kaitlin was an errant child skipping school or something to become…well, a bad girl, she supposed. She glanced at Zak, thinking for the first time that there were certainly worse things. Like pompous, arrogant boyfriends who insisted on nasty wine and steak leather for dinner.

Ernesto managed to look dissatisfied with Kaitlin's career choices as well, but she wanted to be an auditor not a public accountant. There was a different test she had in mind, but for now she wanted to get some experience. It was her life and her choice, wasn't it?

Besides, the test she wanted to take was expensive and so was all the study material she'd need to pass it. She didn't have Daddy paying for everything like Brooke did. Her stepfather was a decent enough guy. He treated her mother very well, but Kaitlin had never wanted or accepted any financial help from him. None.

She'd earn her own way, thank you very much.

Ernesto started a mild rant about how Kaitlin should do a lot of things differently with her life and her career, every word of which she resented. To remain civil to their host, she kept nodding like she cared what he thought and put bites of cheesecake in her mouth to keep from having to respond.

Glancing at Zak, she saw that for the first time all evening he didn't seem to be paying any attention to her or Ernesto. Instead, his focus was on an angry man intently making his way toward them from the direction of the kitchen.

Ernesto was still talking endlessly about all her poor life choices when the newcomer got within eight feet of their table, and screamed. "Ernesto Montego, you fucking bastard! I've come to make you pay for your sins."

The man lurched forward, a gun-filled hand coming from beneath his jacket as he squared his body to take aim.

CHAPTER 14

Zak timed his response to the gun-wielding stranger perfectly. The man wanting Ernesto Montego to pay for his sins smelled like a brewery, but might be able to manage to shoot an innocent bystander in the close quarters of the restaurant. Where the fuck was Ernesto's detail? He'd seen the one guy earlier in the hallway leading to the bathroom area and assumed the one he'd seen in the lobby was stationed outside somewhere.

As Mr. Unhappy leveled the gun at Ernesto's head, Zak moved easily from the table and launched himself at the gunman. Before forward momentum slowed him, Zak shoved the man's elbow straight up. The gun fired toward the ceiling. A puff of plaster rained down on them, tiny pieces plinking into their glasses and on their plates.

In the next second, screams from the other guests filled the room along with the sound of toppling chairs and shattering glass as everyone tried to escape the restaurant en masse.

Zak clamped his hand around the gun and easily ripped it from the drunk man's grasp, pushing him down with a quick shove of his boot to the back of the guy's knees to subdue him.

Ernesto hadn't panicked, only let out a loud grunt of disapproval when the gun fired. He looked around for his men as soon as Zak neutralized the threat. Brooke managed to slide her entire body under the table. Zak wished Kaitlin had joined her, but she'd remained upright, spine ramrod straight, and stared wide-eyed at him.

Zak registered her awe-filled expression, and considered it reward enough for what he'd done.

When the man tried to get up, Zak pushed his neck to the ground, leaning a knee in the center of his back to keep him down.

That was when Ernesto's bodyguards showed up.

Ernesto blamed them immediately. "Where were you, cowards? This man almost killed me."

"Sorry, sir, we didn't see him come in."

Zak was relieved that the bodyguard he'd recognized at the Devil's Playground didn't seem to recognize him. He processed the small victory in his head, despite his reservations. The guy could still remember him later.

Zak spoke up in defense of the bodyguards to win them points. "The guy came from the kitchen area. Maybe your guards didn't see him."

"Well, they should have," Ernesto said with quiet anger. The wail of a lone siren pealed in the distance. The local cops were probably still five minutes out.

Keeping his knee firmly planted in the gunman's back, Zak asked Ernesto, "You want to just hand this guy over to the local police when they get here, or something else?" A louder siren joined the first. "If it's something else, we need to dispose of him before those sirens get here."

Ernesto seemed startled that he was being given a choice. He opened his mouth, then closed it. He stared down at the squirming man beneath Zak's knee.

"Let the local authorities handle it. There were

enough witnesses in here that saw this unprovoked attack."

"You should be dead, Ernesto! You deserve to die for what you did!" the man called out from the floor.

"Shut up," Zak said, pressing down harder. Given the evening he and Kaitlin had just endured from the most conceited man in existence, he wanted to give the guy a medal for his attempt, but saving Ernesto Montego's life in a room full of witnesses would offer Zak a whole different level of cred in his undercover world.

The first two police officers came in screaming for them all to put their hands in the air. The gun he'd snatched from the guy on the floor was in his right hand. The two bodyguards also had their weapons out.

The three of them put their weapons on the floor, but Zak kept the shooter pinned to the ground. After a short clarification from the restaurant manager, the gunman was arrested and placed in official custody. They spent the next two hours giving witness statements before leaving as they'd arrived, in the limo.

This time they had to share it with Ernesto and Brooke.

Zak and Kaitlin entered first, sliding along the far-side bench perpendicular to the premium back seats they'd used on the trip to the restaurant. Ernesto had fired the two bodyguards despite Zak's efforts. They both left as soon as the police released them. Ernesto made a phone call that resulted in a long, heated conversation. By the time they walked out of the restaurant, two new guards had arrived. One guy was currently seated with his back against the wall separating the driver from the backseat.

Zak assumed the other new guard rode up front with the driver.

Surprisingly, Ernesto seemed humbled by Zak's heroics and offered him whatever he wanted in return for saving his life. Zak couldn't very well say he only wanted to bring down his friend's extensive criminal enterprise, so instead he pretended like it was nothing and he'd been happy to do it, etcetera, etcetera.

Ernesto insisted he'd repay the favor one day. Zak would have loved to mention Demarco's name, but couldn't think of a way that it wouldn't sound contrived.

How could he feasibly know about Ernesto's association with Demarco? It was better to let that association unfold naturally later on.

Ernesto wouldn't forget what he'd done, mostly because there had been a room full of witnesses and the man cared deeply about what other people thought.

Tonight's events afforded Zak a firm stroke in the atta-boy column for when he and Demarco, and Miles, went into business. He'd have to remember to be shocked to learn that Ernesto and Demarco were business partners. Perhaps he'd remark about it being a small world. Whether Miles knew about tonight probably didn't matter given what had ultimately happened, but Zak looked forward to telling him about it.

They arrived at Kaitlin's house in no time, although he was very ready to say goodnight to Ernesto and his gigantic ego. Watching Kaitlin's jaw tighten throughout the evening whenever Ernesto was talking—which was most of the time—made Zak feel for her even more. Both of them would likely require surgical help to unclench their faces, which had been clamped down to keep the evening's peace.

"I hope you don't mind if I keep your stepsister for a little while," Ernesto said as the driver opened the limo's back door. "Brooke and I are going out for a night cap at my hotel."

Kaitlin managed to unhinge her jaw and say, "I don't mind at all."

Ernesto got out first, presumably to ease their exit

from the vehicle. Kaitlin said goodnight to Brooke over her shoulder, but didn't wait for any response before practically leaping out of the vehicle. To be fair, none was given, because Brooke's gaze focused entirely on Zak the moment Ernesto got out of the vehicle.

"Nice to have dinner with you, Zak," she said under her breath as he moved past. She patted his ass twice. It was a pretty ballsy move, given the identity of her boyfriend and the fact his new bodyguard was sitting right there.

Zak did not respond or acknowledge Brooke's overture in any way. Kaitlin grabbed his hand and tucked up next to him like her life depended on it.

"Don't wait up," Ernesto said with an exaggerated wink.

"The truth is, I won't even be there," Kaitlin said, squeezing Zak's fingers as if he'd dare disagree in Ernesto's presence. "Brooke will have the house to herself tonight if she wants it, right, Zak?"

Zak allowed half his mouth to curl upward, as if acknowledging the coming evening with Kaitlin alone at his place.

Ernesto slapped the center of Zak's back a couple of times way too hard, and climbed into the limo without another word. Good riddance to them both.

Hand in hand, and without looking back, Zak led Kaitlin up the front walk to his porch. He unlocked the door, but once he stepped inside, Zak felt like something was off. He sensed a presence in the room and moved in front of Kaitlin as she tried to follow him in.

He reached for the foyer light to turn it on as a voice asked, "Was that *Ernesto Montego* getting into that limo outside?"

The chandelier overhead illuminated Miles's shocked expression. Behind him, Kaitlin moved closer, pressing into his back like he was her new hiding place.

"What are you doing here?" Zak asked, arching one brow in a show of contempt.

"I need to talk to you." Miles flashed a grin, moving backward into the living room space. He nodded once in Kaitlin's direction as if to say, "Ditch the girl so we can have a long conversation."

Zak turned to face Kaitlin as Miles melted further into the darkness of the living room. "Why don't you head home, baby? I'll call you when I'm through."

Her gaze moved upward toward his room briefly. She whispered, "Can't I just wait for you upstairs?"

He shook his head and opened the front door wider. "Better if this conversation can't be overheard by anyone, right?"

"This isn't the end of our evening, is it?" she asked, stepping onto the front porch, but looking extremely unhappy about it.

Zak followed her out and closed the door behind him. He took her into his arms and kissed her like he'd wanted to all night long. Breaking the kiss too soon, he said, "I'll call you in a little while."

"Do you prom—" She stopped speaking as quickly as she'd started. "I mean, do you swear?"

Zak fought the urge to laugh. She was the very definition of adorable. "Yes. I swear I'll call."

"Okay. I'll be waiting for you."

He released her, watching until she'd walked all the way across their shared driveway to *her* front porch. When she finally disappeared around the corner, he stepped back into his house. Leaving the living room lights off, he sat himself in the comfortable recliner and flipped the television on for noise.

Miles was seated in the room's darkest corner near the fireplace. "So was it?" he asked.

"Was it what? I mean to say, what the *fuck*, Miles?"

Miles pushed out a long sigh of exasperation. "How

did you end up sharing a limo with Ernesto Montego?"

"Kaitlin's sister invited the two of us out to dinner with her *new* boyfriend." Zak clicked the remote, channel surfing until he found a sports channel showing a baseball game.

"I see. Well, did you make a good impression? That might come in handy later."

Zak shook his head and laughed, wondering at the timing of his good fortune. "In fact, I saved his life from a gun-wielding psycho in front of a whole room full of witnesses at the restaurant."

"Shut the fuck up!"

"I was going to call you the minute I got home."

Miles huffed. "No you weren't. You were going to fuck the blonde again—not that I blame you. Turns out she really *is* hot."

"Why don't you shut your mouth about her right now," Zak said in a quiet, matter-of-fact tone, fiddling with the remote again, giving up on hopes of seeing a game and trying to find a station with a rundown of the day's sports scores.

"You don't get to keep her. You know that right?"

"Whatever. I can't ditch her until this thing is resolved with Demarco. He thinks we're a couple. We're playing it that way."

"Oh, are you? Quite the sacrifice you're making, Zak. I'll have to put you in for an award or something."

"Fuck you. Why are you even here?"

"We got the early ballistics report back from Julio's crime scene, which was a fuckin' mess, by the way. After they killed him with a shot to the heart, they fired a shotgun blast into his face. Fuckers really like to make a point, don't they?"

"Yes. They do." Zak's stomach sank. A messy scene like that implied fury or possible betrayal if Demarco had been responsible. What might Julio have told them before he was gunned down? Zak hadn't exactly been forthcoming with Julio about his past after meeting Demarco that first time.

Julio had been approached because of his familial ties to Demarco's group. Zak had been placed in the garage for an introduction, which he'd procured through Julio. If Julio knew he wasn't a criminal, Zak hadn't been the one to tell him. He wondered who'd ratted Julio out.

"However, the 9mm fatal bullet to the chest was traced to a surprising place."

"Do tell."

"Funny coincidence. Registration came back on a stolen gun."

"Not so shocking."

"Yeah. But it was pinched from someone identified as a known associate of Ernesto Montego. And another reason I stepped in tonight."

Zak turned his head and looked at his handler-turned-business partner. "That's worrisome."

"I agree. What are the chances of that?"

"Zero percent of zilch."

"Exactly."

"What the fuck is going on here? How are Julio's murder and Ernesto Montego's sudden appearance here in town connected?"

"Only way I can think of is our mutual psycho dealer, Demarco, but this came up fast. Until last night, no one had Demarco tied to Montego."

"Which is even more worrisome."

"Right-o. This is a dangerous setup, Zak, and getting more dangerous by the minute."

"So what's the plan?"

"The money in the blonde's backyard shed is clean. There's no way to trace it back to The Organization or to where it will go when spent by criminals, meaning our initial plan is completely out the window."

"Are you going to take Demarco and Montego down at the same time?"

"Yes, if possible. But we need clear intent. And we need them to say criminal stuff out loud."

"Which will take a fuckin' miracle."

"It's all we have. So, we'll all be wired at the meeting tomorrow, but it's a remote system. The techies'll turn it off at first for the scans, then we signal them and they turn the tapes on."

"Dangerous."

"You weren't promised unicorns shooting sunshine and rainbows out of their asses with this job, were you?"

Zak stifled a smile. "Whatever. I'll let you see yourself out, but keep in mind that Demarco is probably still having me followed."

"I know."

"Of course you do. I'll secure the money and meet you tomorrow at the warehouse. I'm hoping you will send me a more detailed plan for what the fuck we're doing before then."

"Yeah, I hope that happens, too."

He left the television on and waved at Miles without looking, assuming he'd exit in the same sneaky way he'd come in.

Zak went out the side door that led directly to Kaitlin's backyard, which was also hidden from the street. He wanted to ensure the money was truly in her shed. The small, squat corrugated-metal building was up against the fence. An untrimmed tree from a neighbor's yard hid half the structure with low-hanging branches. That came in very handy for his purposes.

This late at night, it was likely no one could see him, not even Kaitlin. He used his picks on the shed's lock. Inside, the money wasn't even hidden. *Shit*. What if Kaitlin had come in here? A double-sided leather motorcycle saddlebag was in the wheelbarrow perched against the left side of the shed, as if it had been thrown in haphazardly. He unbuckled one of the pouches and pulled back the flap. Fat stacks of cash were stuffed inside.

Quietly and carefully, Zak hid the bags in a cardboard box behind the wheelbarrow, well out of sight if anyone poked their head inside. Not exactly under lock and key, but hopefully it would work in the short term. He closed up the shed and headed for Kaitlin's back door. It occurred to him that he should have counted it, but he didn't want to take the chance of being seen rifling around in there until he had to. He'd move the money in the morning.

He knocked sharply, not caring if anyone could see him. He was impatient to get inside and explain things to her. He didn't even know what he'd say, but hoped inspiration would strike when he needed it. Zak pounded on Kaitlin's back door again, not wanting to traipse to the front door.

There was a long pause before the curtain opened slightly. She peered out at him, frowning, but unlocked the door.

He let himself inside her darkened kitchen and closed and locked the door, only to turn and see she'd obviously been crying. A lot. *Fuck*.

CHAPTER 15

"I didn't expect you," Kaitlin said, hiccupping only once. The minute she'd come home, she'd waited for one of two things. For Zak to call or her sister to return to the house and realize she wasn't spending the night with Zak, but sitting alone waiting foolishly by the phone for him to call.

"Why not? I swore to you I'd be here."

She shrugged, sucking in a deep breath to hold back more tears.

His brows furrowed. "You should know that I take that shit seriously. Why the tears, baby?" At least he looked upset that she'd been crying. He took a step closer. She folded her arms across her middle as some idiotic barrier to keep him at bay.

In retrospect, it was foolish for her to be weeping like a little girl or a virgin over his quick dismissal earlier. Of course he had a life beyond their *fake* relationship. She hadn't seen the other man very well. Likely that had been on purpose. All the secrecy made her nervous. She was a straight arrow. She hadn't ever gotten so much as a parking ticket.

Plus, she didn't know what Zak did besides work at the garage, which was also a problem. Did he have shady connections with disreputable people? Mr. Demarco certainly looked the part, but she was back to stereotyping again. Perhaps they were selling dental equipment to each other. The thought lightened her mood slightly.

If Zak was a criminal—as her sister had implied more than once—she didn't know that she should remain in any kind of liaison with him, erotic or not.

Too bad she'd already fallen in love with the bad boy next door with too many sketchy friends. She knew herself. She'd do almost anything to win him over and keep him in her life on a permanent basis, regardless of his extra-curricular activities.

Honestly, the tears had been because she'd been more worried about her stepsister showing up after cavalierly saying, "You can have the house to yourself," only to discover that maybe that wasn't going to be true after all. That maybe Zak would never call her again or show up in her life, which had made her cry harder.

Insecurity was a vile, insidious affliction.

Kaitlin backed up a step, widening the gap between them. "I was afraid Brooke was going to beat you here."

"Oh?" He took a long step forward. He was only an arm's length away now. "What difference does that make?"

"I believe I told you how mean she can be."

He huffed. "She was certainly nasty at dinner."

"Yes. She was." Kaitlin had been studying his chest, but looked up when he acknowledged her stepsister as being a shit.

Softening, she said, "I'm glad I wasn't the only one who noticed. Usually she hides it better when we're with our parents."

"No doubt. But I'm not that important. And she was trying to play off her new boyfriend, Mr. Pompous. I'll bet she's a real piece of work any time of the day or night." He took another step closer. She wouldn't have to move far to touch him.

"I figured she'd make fun of me for being unable to keep a bad boy like you interested for very long."

"Well, she'd be completely wrong, wouldn't she? Here I am. Very interested."

Unfolding her arms, she put a hand on his chest and asked, "Why did you come to the back door?"

He grinned. "Is that why it took you so long to answer? Were you watching out the front window for me instead?" Another half step put him toe to toe with her bare feet. The heat radiating from his body warmed her, and he smelled so good.

"No comment." But she smiled.

He put his hand over hers, squeezing her fingers gently. "In answer to your question, I did it for our limited privacy."

"Is that the truth?"

"Yes. Maybe I didn't want any of our nosey neighbors seeing me come to your front door this late at night, or worse, see you coming back to my place. You know how small-town folks can talk."

"And that's really why?"

He moved closer, crowding her against the counter by the stove. He leaned in, bending down until his lips were a whisper away from hers. "Yes," he said quietly. "What else could it be?"

That you were too ashamed of me, she thought.

Kaitlin expected him to kiss her. He didn't. He waited, holding himself just shy of touching.

After several breathless seconds on her part, Kaitlin pushed her mouth against his, licking her way inside, wanting him to respond. And in a millisecond—boy howdy—he did. It must have been exactly what he was waiting for.

The moment she instigated the kiss, he overwhelmed

her as he always did, plundering her lips, ratcheting her lust to higher levels with each stroke of his tongue within her mouth.

He lifted her up. Her ass cheeks hit the edge of her counter, right before he guided her legs apart. Before she realized what had happened, he'd stepped between her thighs to press his thickening cock against her moistening center quite intimately.

She wrapped her legs around him, but he unfolded them, breaking the kiss. She was about to ask why, but figured it out when he started kissing her throat and then her chest and then her belly.

The slinky dress she still wore was bunched around her thighs, courtesy of Zak's clever hands. He was also able to pull her panties off without much effort. When he buried his face between her thighs, her body arched. She banged the back of her head on the cabinet holding all her cooking spices. How appropriate. This was about to be a very spicy scene.

But he stopped, stood up and scooped her into his arms. He carried her easily as he mounted the stairs. "Which one is your room?" She pointed and he moved quickly into her bedroom.

Once inside, and without much fanfare, he dropped her in the center of her bed with her legs dangling off the side, fell to his knees and resumed what he'd started in the kitchen.

Before dinner, on her dining room table no less, he'd brought her to the height of ecstasy until she screamed his name to the rafters. Now he seemed intent on a repeat, only using his tongue instead of his fingers. Hadn't he also promised that? She couldn't remember.

It didn't take long for him to bring her off with his tongue. He was like a master playing a crafted instrument when it came to her body. Kaitlin started to scream his name in orgasmic release.

After several minutes of breathing hard, Zak asked, "Am I forgiven for earlier?"

"Yes," she managed to gasp. "And if you let your beard grow out for a few days and do that again, I'll be even more forgiving."

He nipped her inner thigh. "Noted."

Zak stood up. He paused between her open legs, gazing up and down her body.

"What are you thinking?"

He grinned. "Honestly? I'm thinking about several different sexual positions and the next one I'd like to try out with you."

Kaitlin leaned up on her elbows. "You know what I want to try?"

"Tell me."

"Let me show you." Feeling like the baddest bad girl of them all, Kaitlin flipped over onto her stomach, rose up on all fours, whipped her hair over her shoulder and followed that action with a saucy look. "Can you guess yet?"

Zak moved forward, grabbed her hips, and pulled her into his body. They didn't quite line up, but that could be fixed if he'd just climb onto the bed behind her.

"Are you certain this is what you want to try?" Zak bent and kissed the bare skin at the edge of her low-backed dress. The tone of his voice had gone lower.

"Yes. This is what I want."

"I'll be able to penetrate you even deeper. Are you ready for that?"

"Yes. Perfect," she fairly purred.

He pulled her from the bed until she was on her feet, turned her around and helped her remove the sexy, slinky dress. Then she undressed him. She pulled open the night stand to show him the condoms she had available. He took one and put it in place. She helped.

He cupped her face in his palms and kissed her like

she was the rarest creature on earth. Like maybe he was honored to be part of her life. Like he was falling in love with her, just like she'd already fallen in love with him. It was a nice dream and Kaitlin clung to it.

Before she knew it, they were writhing on top of the bed, kissing and touching and moaning. Kaitlin was fired up after only a few minutes. She was the one who broke the endless kiss to get into position on all fours to experience the next new position.

She grabbed the top of her padded headboard and thrust her butt against his groin. His sheathed cock felt enormous against her, but she was so ready to join with him.

True to his word, the moment he entered her, she was filled to the very brink of capacity. As wet as she already was from kissing him as they rolled around on the bed and her earlier climax, there was absolutely no pain, only pleasure and lots of it.

Zak held her hips, his fingers digging into her flesh with purpose as he thrust in and out of her body wildly. He was right. It did feel deeper. He kept up the rhythm until she felt him push his hand between her legs and stroke her, ensuring her climax. It only took four rubs until she came apart screaming. Zak lasted quite a bit longer, which also felt amazing in the aftermath of her recent orgasm.

His arms wrapped around her torso, hands palming her breasts for his final few thrusts until he grunted and slammed deeply inside one last time.

With his face buried in the back of her neck as he climaxed, she heard Zak clearly whisper, "I love you, Kaitlin."

Zak's eyes practically rolled back in his head the

moment his epic release consumed him. Thrusting inside her very tight body from behind was hands-down his favorite position, and never more so than with his sweet Kaitlin suggesting it first. She was perfect. The best woman he could have ever asked for.

He clutched her to him, thinking about how foolish it was to have fallen in love with her. But he had. No denying it now. The words, *I love you, Kaitlin*, danced in his head, banging around until he wanted to scream them to the heavens.

Kaitlin disengaged from him, turned in his arms and kissed him hard on the mouth. "I love you, too," she said and kissed him again. Whoa. Had she just read his mind?

"What?"

"You said you loved me. Well, you whispered it, but I heard you. I wanted you to know that I love you, too." She laughed, kissed him on the mouth again, and bounced out of bed.

Had he said that very dangerous phrase out loud? Obviously.

His feelings aside, Zak found it difficult to be sorry about expressing how he felt about her. It was the truth. He only worried about how complicated a future with her would be. In fact, he wasn't even certain one was possible. *You don't get to keep her,* Miles had reminded him earlier.

Zak followed her to the bathroom to clean up, not denying that he'd expressed his love. Once he left for good, she might not be as happy about his declaration or forgiving if he could manage to return to her one day.

He coaxed her back to bed with amazing kisses, made love to her a second time, front to front because he wanted to watch her face as he moved inside her body. She didn't disappoint him, being very expressive as he loved her, never once holding back.

She clung to him, her nails digging deliciously into

the muscles along his spine as they both recovered. Once his breathing slowed to a normal level, he moved to go for the bathroom to clean up. She held fast. "Don't leave me yet."

"I'm just going to the bathroom, baby." She released him, and he disappeared into her en suite. When he climbed back beneath the sheets, she fastened herself to him solidly, tangling her legs with his as if to make it difficult for him to get away.

"Every time you move from my side I have to force myself not to ask when I'll see you again," she said against his throat.

"I was only gone for a minute." He tried to make light.

"You know what I mean." He remained silent, contemplating the future. When he left in the morning, it was very likely he wouldn't see her again. Should he break it off now, and warn her not to expect him ever again? Or should he remain silent, making a clean getaway tomorrow without discussion? Disavow his love for her even as the words were still fresh in his mind and heart and the very air around them?

A dilemma, for certain, but his assignment for The Organization was clear. Get in, get the job done and get out safely. Dragging a civilian, whether or not he loved her, into this fiasco was not a good idea. Once they arrested Demarco and Montego, his mission would be complete and he'd be on his way.

"I don't know what you want me to say, Kaitlin." He didn't mean to sound brusque, but he felt her stiffen the moment he said her name.

"I want you to stay with me. I want you to *want* to be with me."

"I do want to be with you. But I also have other obligations." *And another name and another life you don't even know about.*

"You're right. I need to know something else, too."

"Yes. I care about you," he said and kissed her shoulder, wishing this discussion hadn't turned away from passion, kissing and sex.

"Why are you meeting with Mr. Demarco?"

After a long silence where he ruminated about what to say, he said, "I'd rather not explain that to you right now."

"Is what you're doing with him in any way against the law?"

"Same answer."

"Does that mean yes?"

"It means I'd rather not explain that to you right now."

"But will you explain some day?"

"No promises."

"I thought promises were for little girls and virgins."

Zak was so frustrated he wanted to tell her the truth, the whole truth, and nothing but the truth, but he was bound by vows he'd made to The Organization. He couldn't explain any more to her. In fact, he'd already said too much.

"Do you want me to leave?" he asked in a quiet, desperate tone.

She stilled, her expression shocked and sad. She responded with a very tiny, "No. I don't." She dropped her gaze and rolled to face away from him.

Zak felt like the hugest shit-heel in the land. He hadn't meant to hurt her feelings.

Snuggling up behind her, he draped an arm over her waist and kissed the back of her neck. "I swear to you that I'm not doing anything illegal with Demarco, but you can't repeat that to anyone, and I'll deny it if you do." She turned her head, but he kept talking. "No. I can't explain everything to you right now, but one day I *swear* that I will. Okay?" *I'll try to anyway.*

Then he added from his heart, "Maybe I need you to have faith in me."

"I do have faith in you." She cuddled back against his body, yawning big like he wanted to. It had been a hell of a night. It was after two in the morning and he had a long day tomorrow.

Kaitlin fell asleep in his arms within a few minutes. Zak followed her into a dream-filled slumber soon after.

Zak woke just before dawn, pulled away from Kaitlin and slowly dressed in the dark as he watched to ensure she slept on.

He didn't remember his dreams precisely, but carried a distinct recollection that his sleep had been very restless, which was an unusual occurrence after two such amazing rounds of sexual bliss.

Typically he slept like the dead after more than one round of sex. But he also remembered that he'd said too much to her the night before. He'd told her he loved her without meaning to say the words out loud. Even though it was true, he shouldn't have admitted it in the heat of the moment.

Worse was swearing he'd explain his acquaintance with Demarco as not being illegal. What the fuck had he been thinking?

Zak rarely had regrets, and in this case his only pause for concern was having Kaitlin involved in any way with Demarco or Montego, although he had her bitchy stepsister to thank for that. And probably something else had plagued his sleep.

He hadn't had a chance to assess her stepsister's relationship with Montego. She'd smacked *his* ass on the way out of the limo. Did Montego know how much of a flirt she was? She'd also stared at him out Kaitlin's window. Was Brooke involved in her boyfriend's business? Did she know who her new boyfriend associated with? Did she care? He tucked all those questions away for later and finished dressing.

He took one last, very long look at Kaitlin sleeping peacefully and exited the room, mentally disassociating himself from any hint of a personal life for the moment. He had a job to do. His feelings, regardless of how profound they were, didn't matter. He crept downstairs to check the perimeter inside and out.

A quick look out several of her front windows along with her front door yielded no one lurking around. No movement. Zak padded quietly back through Kaitlin's house and exited out the kitchen door into the yard on a stealthy path back to the shed. He'd collect the money, hide it at his own house and do his best to keep from having to explain anything to Kaitlin before he had to leave her forever.

He picked open the lock once more, pulled the door closed but unlatched, and retrieved the bags of money. His phone vibrated in his pocket, signaling a text message. A glance at the screen told him it was from Miles. Zak stopped and listened to ensure he was still alone in the area of the shed before checking the message. It was a cryptic note with limited details.

Zak tapped out an unusually long text in return and hit send just as he heard someone right outside the shed, moving closer. Shit. The bag was wide open, revealing half of the money for tonight's deal. He reached down in time to put his hand on the bag, but without further warning, the door was yanked open, and he was revealed practically with his hand in a proverbial cookie jar filled with money instead of sweets.

A shocked Kaitlin greeted him. She seemed very alert for someone he'd seen just yesterday on the verge of comatose before her morning coffee. "What on earth are you doing in here?" Her gaze dropped to the open bag and the fat stacks of cash.

Her eyes went wide. "What is all that money doing in here?"

Zak did not want to tell Kaitlin anything, but was unsure she'd let him get away without some form of an explanation. And what was he going to say? He couldn't tell her the truth. Not yet. Maybe never.

He looked away from her and remained silent, although he knew that wasn't going to fly for very long. Zak flipped the saddlebag's cover back over the money and secured the fastener.

"Answer me," she said rather forcefully. Being the shrewish girlfriend wasn't what he would have expected, but then again, he'd told her last night he wasn't doing anything illegal with Demarco.

"Sorry, baby. I can't do it. Not right now." *Not ever.*

"That's not good enough."

"I swore to you last night that I couldn't explain, but that I would at some point. Now is not that time."

"I don't believe you ever plan to tell me."

"Why not?"

Her gaze went back to the double saddlebag. "That much cash in order to conduct some nebulous deal can't possibly be legal. I'm not stupid."

"Baby—"

"Don't 'baby' me," she shouted. "What is all that money for?"

CHAPTER 16

Zak's expression went from conciliatory to hard in a millisecond. "I'm not explaining myself to you at this time," he said in a low, dangerous tone. He moved forward, gesturing for her to get out of his way or get mowed over.

Kaitlin backed up until he exited her shed. He turned and re-attached the padlock, snapping it closed. How had he gotten in there in the first place?

"Did you pick the lock on my shed?"

"No comment."

"That is an unacceptable answer."

"Well, it's the best I can do."

Tears welled in her eyes, more in anger than sadness. "You can trust me."

When he moved to face her once more, he stared at her for a long time; his varying expressions seemed at war with one another. Finally, he said, "I've got to take care of something at my house. If you'd like to have breakfast with me, come on over."

"And if I don't?"

He shrugged. "That's up to you."

"Will you explain what's going on?" She pointed to the saddlebags slung over his shoulder.

He paused, looked straight into her eyes and said firmly, "Nope."

"Then no thank you. I'll make my own breakfast."

"Really?" He seemed genuinely surprised that she didn't want to be part of his criminal enterprise without explanation. "I thought last night was special." How did he manage to look hurt? She couldn't blindly trust, could she? What if he was a criminal?

"So did I." Her gaze went from his face to the bags of money again. "But I find that with the almost morning sun I need more information before I continue down this path with you blindly."

He stared at her for several seconds as if coming to some silent decision. He shrugged. "Suit yourself. I'm making fried eggs, bacon and buttered toast. I'm pretty good at it, too."

"How can you be so blasé about this?"

"About what?"

"About these secret meetings you're having with Mr. Demarco and about...us."

"For the record, I'm not blasé. I'm careful. I'm also not the one who lacks faith." His expression hardened. Without further ado, he started walking toward the gate to his yard.

Kaitlin watched him go, but couldn't follow. She'd never seen so much cash in her life. It *had* to be for illicit business. The fact that he wouldn't deny it was another red flag she couldn't ignore. Maybe she did lack faith. It wasn't like anyone had ever proven to be completely devoted to her, especially not any men from her past. He was a bad boy, but after spending time with him she had expected him to be different. Perhaps she was naive.

The gate swung closed with rigid finality, shutting down what Kaitlin had hoped was a special, budding relationship.

She pressed her lips tighter to keep from sobbing and

hurried to her back door. In her kitchen, she fell to her knees and let the dam burst, crying until she couldn't make any more tears. She wasn't certain how long she spent slumped against the cabinets by the back door, but the sun had risen high enough to light up the room.

The front doorbell rang, startling her. Was it Zak? Had he come to make peace? She jumped up and ran to the sink, splashing cold water on her face to cool her likely blotchy red skin and hopefully hide the fact she'd been crying.

The doorbell sounded again and again, echoing through her house. Someone was impatient. She smiled, taking it as a good sign. He was anxious to mend things. He wanted to explain.

She hadn't ruined everything.

She raced to the front door, her robe whipping behind her like a cape. He'd be sheepish. He'd say he missed her at breakfast. He'd give her that special, intense bad boy look right before he kissed her socks off.

Kaitlin unlocked, unbolted and threw open the door.

"It took you long enough," the visitor said, pushing past her into the foyer.

It wasn't Zak.

It was Brooke.

Kaitlin leaned out the front door, looking in the direction of Zak's house, wishing for him to round the corner and offer to make up.

Behind her, Brooke asked, "What are you doing? Come inside."

She heard Zak's motorcycle start up. He revved the engine a couple of times, like he always did right before he drove off. He pulled out of their shared driveway without turning his head in her direction. When he rode away, he didn't look back.

Tears welled in her eyes again.

"Kaitlin, come inside right now," Brooke said, her

compassion clearly absent. She hadn't commented on Kaitlin's appearance, at least not yet. In this singular case it was a good thing her stepsister was so self-absorbed.

She closed and locked the front door. Turning toward her stepsister, Kaitlin asked, "What are you doing here so early?"

Brooke headed for the stairs, also without looking back. *Am I invisible?* "All of my things are here. I ended up staying the night at Ernesto's hotel room." Her stepsister sounded smug, as usual, but for the first time in ever, Kaitlin didn't care. She could be smug, too.

"It's a good thing," she said, following Brooke up the steps. "Zak and I ended up spending the night here instead of at his house. Likely you wouldn't have gotten much sleep here."

Brooke laughed, hitting the landing's top step and heading toward the guest room. "Well, I didn't get much sleep in Ernesto's hotel suite either."

Kaitlin wasn't planning on mentioning the morning disagreement. She followed Brooke down the hall, turning into her room as her stepsister moved the opposite way across the hall.

"Have you had coffee yet?" Brooke called out over one shoulder.

"No. But let me get dressed and I'll go down and make a pot for us." She closed the door to her room. Greeting her were the tangled sheets from the night before. She smelled Zak in the room and fought the urge to cry again. She inhaled deeply, shook off her sorrow and vowed to take the high road.

Just because he hadn't opened up to her yet didn't mean he wouldn't later on. Her tummy rumbled. Perhaps shrewish girlfriend hadn't been the right move to make by the shed. Perhaps she should have had more faith in him. If she had, her belly would be filled with bacon, eggs and toast courtesy of the bad boy next door.

With Brooke's unexpected appearance this morning, Kaitlin was having serious second thoughts about their argument. She hadn't been fully awake. She hadn't had coffee. Hadn't slept the requisite number of hours she usually did in favor of tangling her sheets with Zak all night long. Zak had whispered that he loved her. The memory of his unexpected words came barging into her head all of a sudden.

A loud noise from the guest room interrupted her reverie. Time always gave her a better perspective. Kaitlin might be involved with an affirmed bad boy, but her stepsister was dating an arrogant prick. So which one of them should be crying?

Not to mention the fact that someone had tried to kill Brooke's boyfriend the night before despite the two bodyguards he'd had with him. She'd assumed having two burly guys following him around were simply for his ego. Given the time she'd spent with him, the shooter's possible motivation might not be coming from left field. To be fair, being a pompous asshole wasn't grounds to be shot by a wild gunman during dinner.

Zak had saved Ernesto from that gunman. Did a bad boy go out of his way to save a man who'd forced them to drink nasty wine and eat steak leather? Hers did.

Begging the question, was he her bad boy still? She hoped so. She eyed her phone on the nightstand, wanting to call him and make nice. She didn't know where he'd gone so early in the morning.

Kaitlin pulled on a pair of her favorite jeans, grabbed an oversized T-shirt and headed back downstairs to make coffee and scrounge for breakfast food. Her brain hurt trying to figure out the ramifications of the ever-changing past twenty-four hours.

She passed by the window she always spied on Zak

from and couldn't help but peek out. Whenever he returned, Kaitlin decided, she'd go over and apologize. She'd plead caffeine deficiency as the reason she was such a bitch this morning. Perhaps they could have make-up lunch. Perhaps she'd surprise him with a blowjob. It was next on her list of sexual things to try.

Before she got as far as her kitchen, there was a loud knock at the front door. She glanced out the side window. Zak's bike was still gone, meaning it was someone new. Then she realized it was Saturday and there could be any number of people standing outside her door, from mobile tree trimming services to Girl Scouts selling cookies.

A smile shaped her lips as she unlocked the door and opened it wide.

That smile froze on her face as the identity of her visitor registered. The beautiful, dangerous demon grinned back, sticking his foot in the door before she could close it.

CHAPTER 17

Zak rode away from his rental house, the heavy, rich, double breakfast he'd consumed churning in his belly. Convinced Kaitlin would change her mind and show up for breakfast, Zak had made extra food, then eaten all of it when it became clear she was *not* going to come over or generate any faith, for that matter.

Truthfully, she'd given him an out insofar as he wasn't supposed to explain his actions or details of his missions to anyone outside of his chain of command in The Organization, let alone a love interest he shouldn't even have.

He'd hoped to skirt the truth enough in the end to satisfy her curiosity. But then again, he also didn't expect he'd speak to her after tonight anyway.

In the back of his mind, he knew this was better.

Clean break. No ties. No regrets.

Now if he could only persuade his heart not to feel so devastated. There was one bright spot. Miles would be happy. Damn it. His undercover handler had sent Zak another cryptic text on his secret phone as he made breakfast. Listed was a time and location to discuss the details of the coming mission. He hoped there was a good plan this time around.

Zak's first stop was the garage to pick up his pay. Eddie felt he was doing his employees a service by not providing funds on Friday night like many other places. He reasoned anyone unhappy with the practice would thank him for not being able to drink their paycheck away on Friday night.

"People have better perspective on Saturday morning when it's time to shake off their Friday night hangover, get the groceries and do chores," he explained when asked. Eddie the Philosopher was likely right.

His face was uncharacteristically somber when he handed Zak the envelope with a weeks' worth of cash. "I hate to be the one to tell you this, since you were friends and all, but Julio was in an accident. He didn't make it."

"What?" Zak was genuinely shocked. He'd expected the Feds to keep a lid on Julio's death for a few days. "What kind of accident?"

"He drove his motorcycle off an embankment, cracked it up. He was a mess. Trust me, it'll be a closed-casket service." Eddie shook his head sadly. He looked down at the envelope he held with Julio's name on it. "Guess I'll give this to his mother."

"His mother?" Another surprise. Zak had thought Julio was all alone in the world. No family. No girlfriend. No one.

"Yeah. I'm pretty sure he had to move in with her after getting out of the joint that last time." He pointed in a northerly direction out of the office door. "She's the one who called to let me know about what happened to him." Eddie coughed a couple of times, clearly upset about having to face Julio's mother with her son's last earnings.

Zak kept his features bland and pointed at the envelope. "Want me to drop that off for you?"

Eddie shook his head. "Nah. I'll take care of it this afternoon."

Zak backed away, but Eddie added, "Hey, Zak. On Monday you'll finish that bike Julio was working on first thing, okay?"

"Sure." Zak wasn't actually planning on being here Monday. This was one of the things he hated about undercover work. Whether it was a good situation or a bad one, leaving abruptly when the job was done never sat well with him. It was like living only part of a life and then abandoning it before finishing things up. He knew it left some innocent people wondering what the hell had happened to him.

Kaitlin's face appeared front and center in his mind. Zak blinked away the vision, got back on his bike and rode out of town, past the Devil's Playground and several miles into the barren landscape of southern Arizona. He needed to clear his head before his meeting with Miles.

Zak drove for a long stretch without passing a single other vehicle. He did a U-turn and gunned the engine heading back the way he'd come to ensure no one had followed him, then turned onto a narrow dirt road. The landscape was dotted with lots of green for this part of the state, giving him even better cover the further he drove away from the main highway.

Four miles of surprisingly smooth terrain later, he took a left at the fork in the road, traversing slightly narrower and bumpier trail. This led to a surprisingly large cabin tucked away behind a long ago landslide that concealed the structure well.

Zak parked his bike out of sight and climbed up the stairs and entered the screened porch. He rapped a knuckle on the sliding glass door leading into a small den with a television going and slid it open.

Miles held up a bottle of water before tossing it in his direction. "You're late."

"No, I'm not."

"Almost."

"Fuck off."

Miles laughed and gestured him inside the surprisingly cool house.

"Figured out a plan for tonight yet?" Zak took a long swig of water as he walked to the dining room, where the mission paperwork, pictures, and details had been set up.

"Maybe." *This meant yes.*

Zak glanced at his watch, trying to calculate if he'd have enough time to see Kaitlin before the warehouse meeting with Miles, Demarco and Montego this evening.

"Got a date?" Miles asked.

"Nope."

"Good. Did you break it off with her?"

"No. She broke it off with me."

That seemed to catch Miles by surprise. "Why?"

Zak blew out a long sigh. "She caught me taking the money out of her shed before dawn this morning. Right after I picked the lock to get into it. Therefore, she wasn't happy and wanted explanations. When I offered breakfast instead of an explanation, she chose not to join me. So I guess we're done."

"Even better. Now you can ride off into the sunset a free man after our meet tonight."

Zak didn't feel like the chains of a relationship were breaking away. Instead, he was miserable. He wanted to see her again. One last time. Checking his watch, he recalculated when he'd have to leave here to fit in a stop at her place before the meeting.

If Miles noticed how often he checked the time while they worked, he didn't remark on it. They mapped out the scenario and a few backup plans if things didn't go according to script.

"I'll already be there when you arrive with your money. We'll show them we have the funds, but insist on inspecting the goods. Nate Salerno is my guy checking the merchandise to ensure it's what we think it is."

"Okay. Who's taking the stuff?"

"Nate will, once we exchange the money and the place is swarmed with cops. We don't want any wannabe big shots from Demarco's crew of losers taking off with the goods in the heat of the arrests."

"Good point."

"The more I think about it, the better I feel about this meet."

Zak nodded. His eye landed on a file folder with Julio's name on it. He picked it up and thumbed through it without really seeing any of the pages.

"Sorry about him, Zak. I wish I knew how he got caught."

"He wasn't even an informant. Just a connection we used to get in." Zak remembered that at least Eddie would give his mother a few dollars. Perhaps he'd also send an anonymous donation to the man's family. He flipped through the file to locate Julio's current address.

"I know we'd planned to give him that status if needed," Miles said. "But he was gone before it even became a topic of discussion."

"Yeah."

Zak paused on a summary of Julio's childhood. An only child, his father had been the founder of the group Demarco now headed. That, Zak knew. He'd gone to prison when Julio was five and died there during a bloody riot between two rival gangs.

He searched for the address again, but saw a notation at the bottom of the page about Julio's mother taking off for parts unknown before he finished high school. Interesting. So who was he living with if not his mother? Or had she come back into his life? He could have been living with anyone, like a grandmother or an aunt or even a baby mama.

"Eddie said Julio's mother called to report his death, but his background says she ran off when he was a teenager. Was that us pretending to be his mother tying up a loose end?"

Miles looked over his shoulder at the file. "Don't know. Maybe she came back and his background was never updated. I can find out and let you know."

"Good. Thanks."

Zak didn't dwell on it. He found the current local address and memorized it for later. The least he could do was pay his respects to Julio's mother if she was still around.

He checked his watch again. If he left right now, he'd have time to stop by Kaitlin's house and say goodbye. Well, he wouldn't say that, but perhaps he could smooth things over at least. He hated the thought of leaving for good while there were bad feelings between them.

Miles huffed. "Take off, already. Go make nice and say goodbye to her, for fuck's sake."

"I'm certain I don't know what you're talking about."

"Whatever. You had a fight with your girl and she broke up with you. Not making nice will roil inside of you forever. You might even be tempted to come back here, going against every rule in our book. So go make your peace. But unless you're going to make her your wife tonight, say goodbye for good. It's the best way."

Married men in The Organization were allowed to share basic knowledge operational status with their wives. Girlfriends? Absolutely not.

Zak grinned at the ludicrous idea of marrying Kaitlin tonight, but was grateful for the chance to see her one last time. "See you at the warehouse."

"Yes, Mr. Pussy-Whipped, you will."

"Fuck off," Zak said, never losing the grin.

"I want your full game face tonight, Zak."

"No problem. You'll have it."

Miles exited the narrow road ahead of Zak until they got to the highway.

Zak let out the throttle on the bike all the way back to town as the sun set in the west revealing a glorious orange and red streaked sky. With the exception of passing Miles driving a black four door sedan a mile out, Zak didn't see anyone else on the road. He roared into the driveway. The curtain didn't so much as twitch in Kaitlin's window. Shit. Maybe she was truly through with him.

He frowned. Her house was completely dark. Perhaps she'd gone out. It was Saturday night. Was she on a date? He ignored the unwelcome feeling in the pit of his stomach *that* thought generated. He swung a leg over his bike to dismount, looking once more over his shoulder at the window, expecting to find her staring at his ass as usual.

The curtain didn't move. Zak pushed out a long breath and headed for his front door. Over the fence to her property, he heard a cat meowing like it was caught in a trap or something. Zak veered to open the unlocked gate leading to Kaitlin's backyard.

The black and white fur ball she'd partially adopted sat on the back porch crying its little cat lungs out. The food bowl she always put out was empty and so was the water dish.

Zak expected the cat to run away as he climbed Kaitlin's back porch stairs, but it didn't. The fluffy little feline started winding around his ankles faster and faster, as if the speedier it went the better its chances of being fed.

"I can't help you, little cat." The cat meowed demandingly and kept threading between his ankles. Perhaps it smelled Kaitlin on him.

He knocked on her back door. A glance at his watch made him pound harder. He only had about ten minutes before he had to leave.

No lights came on. Expecting it to be locked, he turned the door handle anyway. The door swung open. He blocked the cat with his foot and shooed it away when it tried to rush inside. On the counter by the door was a neatly folded bag of cat food. He grabbed it, dumped a pile of dry food in the bowl outside. The cat stopped trying to get inside, buried its little head in the bowl and chomped the food ravenously.

"Kaitlin!" he called out, not wanting to frighten her. "Your back door is unlocked."

Silence. Maybe she'd gone out with her stepsister to avoid running into him.

He bent to fill the cat's water bowl from the spigot by the back door. He'd always enjoyed the view from his bedroom window of *her* bending over to fill the water dish this way.

Once the orphan cat was fed and watered, Zak walked a few more steps into the kitchen, calling her name over and over in louder increments. Nothing.

Zak locked the back door and pulled it closed. He checked under the flowerpot he'd overheard her tell Brooke about. The spare key was there. Good. She could still get in if she'd forgotten her keys.

He wished he could give her hell about leaving her door unlocked. He didn't care how small and safe this town was, no woman living alone should be that trusting. Just consider the reason he was here in the first place. If that didn't say "lock your doors," he didn't know what did.

Zak glanced at his watch one last time. He'd end up being a bit early for the meeting. Whatever. Not seeing Kaitlin before he left weighed on him, but he cast it aside in favor of the takedown. He had a job to do.

As Miles had requested, Zak put his game face on, prepared to arrest bad guys. If everything went according to plan, he and Miles would hand over the money, get the product, Nate would test it and then they'd all be arrested along with Demarco and Montego and their respective forces.

But only Miles and Zak had Get Out Of Jail Free cards.

He roared into the parking lot of the abandoned warehouse prepared to kick asses and take names.

Zak grabbed the saddlebags and headed through the door on the building's north side. Inside, rows of old shelving reaching for the ceiling, empty except for a decade's worth of dust. He walked down the center aisle between the sagging wood and metal shelves, all standing at attention like a recently retired platoon of soldiers. They were old and dusty, but still capable and serviceable.

Hearing voices coming from the opposite end of the warehouse, he picked up his pace. Just before he stepped into the next room beyond the large warehouse filled with dusty shelves, the peal of a woman's laughter made him freeze.

Who the fuck would bring a girlfriend here?

Making a decision, Zak hefted the saddlebags higher on his shoulder and strode confidently through the opening into the next room. Demarco, Montego and Brooke were there. So, Montego was the arrogant prick who'd brought along his girlfriend. Figured. That she was Kaitlin's sister made him a bit uneasy. However, if she ran with dogs, she should expect to get some fleas. She'd go to jail, just like the rest of them.

The back room was not as tall as the warehouse area and it was more cluttered. There were more shelves in either side, but they were smaller and shorter. The group stood in a clearing of sorts surrounded by stacks of wooden pallets that had seen better days and varying levels of boxes. There were a couple tables along the edges of the open space as well.

He didn't see Miles, but his eyes went to another blonde head. He could barely see her, since Demarco and one of his guards blocked his view of the woman. He counted four goons, two for Demarco and two for Montego. Manageable if he had to take them on, but hopefully they'd surrender without a gunfight.

"Zak," Demarco called out jovially. "We have a surprise for you." He snapped his fingers and one of the burly guys behind him shoved the mysterious blonde forward into view.

Mouth trembling and unshed tears welling in her eyes, Kaitlin looked at him with a fear-filled gaze.

Fuck.

CHAPTER 18

Kaitlin had never been as frightened as she was when Zak joined them in the warehouse. It had been a perilously long day fraught with one indignity after another as she was held against her will.

Demarco had not waited for an invitation, but instead muscled his way into her home. She'd asked him to leave, but he'd declined, telling her to behave or her day could get much worse.

Brooke had descended the stairs with her bags packed and looked on as if nothing of note had transpired. Kaitlin felt a pang of guilt that her stepsister was about to be caught up in whatever was happening, but it vanished when Brooke sidled up to Demarco like he was her long lost sugar daddy. She planted a kiss directly on his mouth.

"Are you packed and ready to go, my sweet?" Demarco asked her politely, a shimmer of her lipstick still coating his lower lip.

"Indeed." Brooke solicitously wiped the lipstick stain away with her thumb. Too bad. Kaitlin would have loved to see Ernesto's expression when he discovered Demarco was stepping out with his woman.

"What is going on here?" Kaitlin had backed toward

the kitchen with the idea that maybe she could escape through the back door. Had she locked it after her cryfest? It was a foolish thought, given the cozy way her stepsister and the beautiful demon were acting, but she couldn't help it.

"You're coming with us, sis," Brooke said.

"No, thank you."

Demarco grinned wider. "I'll have to insist."

Through all the rest of her day in captivity, her stepsister had been a total mean girl. From all the conversations she'd overheard, it seemed that Demarco and Ernesto were in league with a third bad guy whose name they hadn't mentioned.

She'd first assumed it was Zak, but then realized they were leading him into some kind of trap. The three conspirators planned to take advantage of him tonight after he paid them. It was likely the same batch of cash that had caused their unfortunate argument this morning.

Did that make Zak a dumb criminal who'd trusted when he shouldn't have? Was he here to stop them? Or was she painting him as a good guy because that's what she wanted him to be? Even so, she clung to that unlikely scenario as her day progressed.

They hadn't tied her up, but had threatened to if she didn't cooperate. They'd fed her and Brooke an elaborate late lunch in a back room. She'd wanted to steal the steak knife to use as a weapon, but there hadn't been an opportunity to get away with it. She had no weapon, nor did she really have the knowledge to use one if she did come across one. She felt pretty useless.

Now that Zak was here, waves of relief washed through her with each step closer he came. It didn't matter that they'd parted on poor terms. He'd take care of her, just like he had at the Devil's Playground.

Although the closer he got, the angrier he looked. Was he angry because she was encroaching on another meeting with Demarco? Did he know she hadn't been given a choice?

Lips trembling, not even knowing what to say, Kaitlin started to explain. "Zak. I—"

"Silence!" Demarco barked, giving her a malevolent stare.

She sealed her lips tight, but her gaze stayed on Zak. His expression was almost sinister, but his focus was Demarco, not her. Small relief, given the circumstances.

"Why did you bring her here?" he asked.

Demarco grinned. "To ensure your cooperation. I was afraid you'd balk at working with Miles at the last moment. She's here only to ensure you hold up your part of the bargain."

Zak snorted. "Too bad we broke up."

"What's this? You broke up with her?" Demarco looked unconcerned with the demise of their relationship. "This calls into question your sanity, my friend." He leered at Kaitlin.

"No. She ended it." His gaze went to the gun Demarco held on Kaitlin and then drilled into the other man's face. "Hard to blame her, given how she's been treated around the people I associate with."

"That may be true, but regardless of your relationship issues, it doesn't change the fact that she holds sway over you. I can see in your eyes right now that you care for her. I can't imagine you'll let any harm come to her, even if she truly stomped on your heart. Her continued safety still ensures your cooperation, does it not?"

Zak's lips shaped into a smile, but his eyes were cold, angry and unwavering from Demarco's. "At this point, I'm hopeful that if I kill you and save her, she'll take me back. Want to get married later, baby?" he asked her with a wink. Kaitlin almost responded. Her eyes widened at the utter surprise of his sudden proposal. *Yes, she wanted to scream. Let's go right now.*

Demarco laughed uproariously. "Big talk for a man not at *all* in control of this situation."

Zak sent his gaze skyward for a second, then changed the subject as he lowered his head. "Where's your boy Miles?" His gaze strayed to Ernesto. "I'd like to finish this deal and get on with my life."

Demarco also looked briefly at Ernesto. "Patience, my friend. I'm certain he's on his way. You're early. If all goes according to my plan, we'll all be rich tonight."

Kaitlin hadn't been too surprised to see Ernesto show up, since Brooke was with her and Demarco. He'd joined them less than half an hour before Zak arrived. Kaitlin would have loved to tell Ernesto about Brooke's kiss with Demarco, but her stepsister threatened to have Zak killed the moment he stepped into the warehouse if she did.

"I promise not to tell," she assured Brooke—all the while thinking promises were for little girls and virgins. She was neither, thanks to Zak.

She was, however, very surprised that Ernesto had kept his pompous mouth shut for so long. Maybe being an arrogant prick was an act he put on when it suited him. She'd gotten the distinct impression at dinner the night before that he and Zak had never met.

Perhaps they were all putting on an act and she was too foolish to recognize any of it.

If Ernesto was surprised to see Zak here for this deal, he didn't show that either. She should probably have *naïve idiot* tattooed on her forehead, unless it was already there in a special ink only visible to those who took advantage of innocents.

Zak's arms had remained by his sides while he traded verbal jabs with Demarco, but all of a sudden he reached up and adjusted the saddlebag slung over his shoulder. He stared intensely into her eyes and tugged his ear. Twice. She squinted, wondering why he was looking at her so hard. Was he actually angry she was here? Did she have sway over him like Demarco intimated? More importantly, did he really want to marry her?

The faint sound of a vehicle arriving outside reached them. Everyone looked in the direction of tires crunching over gravel. Everyone except Zak. He intensified his stare, winked, and tugged his ear again.

Kaitlin abruptly remembered the signals they'd discussed in the limo on their way to the restaurant. He was telling her they needed to leave. She tried to keep her expression from giving away her excitement to the others and nodded slightly. He dropped his arm and seemed to relax. He winked once more and gave her a quick half-smile.

Kaitlin looked toward the sound of quiet footsteps approaching behind her. She saw a man she didn't know, arm lifting slowly with each step he took.

She didn't notice the gun until the barrel was level and pointed in her direction. Kaitlin screamed as he pulled the trigger.

CHAPTER 19

Zak heard the gunshot and Kaitlin's shriek so close together they could have been one sound. He dropped the saddlebags on the floor and launched himself in her direction, already knowing it was too late to push her out of the way if she was the target.

Two more gunshots echoed in the room and Demarco's two men were suddenly sprawled on the ground, not moving.

He grabbed Kaitlin, wrapping her tight in his arms as he dragged her to the floor. He twisted to absorb the fall's impact, feeling her soft, warm curves pressed to his front. *Please, God, no.* He rolled until she was beneath him, shielded by his bulk, and ran his hands over her looking for the wet stickiness of blood. They were mostly covered by a rickety stack of pallets, only their feet were exposed to the direction of the shooter.

"I'm not hit," she said hoarsely, clutching his biceps. "He didn't shoot me."

The overwhelming relief almost made him limp. He looked hurriedly around. Demarco lay on the ground, eyes staring at nothing. Then the bastard blinked and groaned. He closed his eyes, but Zak could see him breathing.

Zak got a glimpse of blue jean-clad legs and work boots, but it wasn't enough to reveal the identity of the shooter. Montego stood nearby, seemingly unperturbed and unafraid of the gunplay.

Kaitlin's arms wrapped around Zak's neck, pulling him close. Her lips brushed his throat with the barest of kisses. Her tone anguished, she said, "I need to tell you. I'm so sorry about this morning."

Love for her filled him. "Don't be. It's all on me. I'm sorry they took you."

Zak did a quick scan of their surroundings, trying to assess what the hell would happen next. "Listen to me. First chance you get, run. Get out of here. Don't look back."

"Only if you're with me. I won't leave you." He stared at her, ready to argue, but couldn't. They'd made up and he wanted to keep it that way. He'd just have to make sure she survived both their stubbornness.

Montego watched them with a smug smile.

"Let's get up," Zak said softly. He inhaled deeply, her unique fragrance settling in his lungs and once more imprinting on his soul as he stood and helped her to her feet.

What would he do to protect her from harm? Anything.

The moment he turned, putting her behind him, she whispered, "And if we escape with our lives tonight, I *will* marry you."

Surprise didn't describe how he felt. Taking a protective stance in front of Kaitlin, Zak gathered his wits and faced the shooter. It took every last shred of his control not to shout, *What the fuck*!

"Surprised to see me, Zak?"

Fuck, yeah, I'm surprised, dude! "Not really. Something was all wrong about the way you died."

Julio took the baseball cap off his head. Zak had

never seen him wear one. It looked as out of place as him being alive.

"It that so? I thought it was rather convincing."

Zak looked down at Demarco and nodded once. His eyes were open again, but he didn't look to be in very good shape. "I don't know. I'd be willing to bet Diego was more surprised than me." *Fuck. What is going on here?*

Julio spat and cursed in Spanish. The wet spittle landed on the center of Demarco's expensive custom shirt near the bloody bullet hole that had brought him down. He needed medical attention, but Julio didn't seem too worried about the man's future. Julio slid a glance toward Kaitlin and smiled. Zak wanted to rip his lips from his face. He stood up straighter.

Julio laughed.

"What's so funny?"

"Watching you valiantly try to save her life when that night in Diego's bar, she saved your ass first."

"What the fuck are you talking about?"

Montego, who'd been unexpectedly silent as a church mouse since Zak arrived, took a step closer into their circle and started talking in that arrogant, annoying tone he'd mastered. "Julio and I have had a long-standing relationship. His father was *patron* of the group Diego now operates…" He trailed off and stared down at Demarco. "I mean, the one he *used* to take care of."

Demarco roused enough to give Montego an evil glare, but seemed to be struggling just to breathe. Montego promptly laughed too long at his own joke. Brooke joined in for a second as if by reflex, but soon quit. She watched Demarco carefully, like someone waiting for a snake to strike. Zak knew personally her proclivities as a flirt. Perhaps he could use that to his advantage.

Zak asked, "I don't understand. What did he do that you needed to kill me for?"

That seemed to be all the opening Julio needed to start ranting. "Fucker ruined everything by going soft and letting his own fucked up interests cloud the way things should have been run." Julio spit on Demarco again, this time hitting his cheek.

Demarco clumsily wiped the spittle off with his inner elbow sleeve. It looked like it cost him. Zak didn't feel sorry for him, but bat-shit crazy Demarco was at least predictable in his own way. Julio was not. This Julio was an unknown entity. He seemed to have Montego's respect as well as managing to mastermind this whole clusterfuck with The Organization none the wiser. And that made him very dangerous.

Crazy and not stupid equaled very dangerous.

Zak mentally scrambled for a way to get Kaitlin out of here. He might have to carry her out over one shoulder, tie her up and head back in, but so be it.

He couldn't believe The Organization's intel had been so wrong, from Julio's role in Demarco's group to the mistaken impression that Julio was well out of the criminal legacy his father had left him. He'd have to discover how their information had been so far off. If he got out of here.

Julio pointed toward Kaitlin. "The night your girlfriend came into the Devil's Playground, I was about to take you out."

"Oh?" Zak noticed that Demarco seemed just as surprised, but Montego nodded like he knew all about it.

"Yeah, man. I'd started moving in, ready to point my gun and blow your head off. I was going to kill first and explain later that I didn't trust you." He glanced at Demarco. "Diego only would have screamed about blood on the fucking pool table, but what the fuck, you know? You were done. Nothing personal, you understand, just a lesson to Diego for not checking you out."

"What?"

"He took my word for you, dude. He should have checked on his own whether you were golden or not. I was planning on taking out Diego when Ernesto showed up." Julio's gaze went to Kaitlin. "But then little Miss Prim and Proper stumbled into the bar like some starry-eyed, lovesick schoolgirl.

"Diego waved me off and I knew the deal wasn't going to be discussed. I could see it in his eyes that he wanted to let things with your girl play out, because he got all fucking dewy over her in an instant." Julio laughed.

"I knew he'd want a film of you fucking her. That's why he sent you into the back office. There's a camera in there. Did you know that? He'd planned to show it to her once he lured her in and fucked her himself. Is that some sick shit or what?"

Zak's belly roiled. "Yep. That's some sick shit, all right. I thought I got hustled out because Ernesto showed up."

Julio shrugged. "Ernesto was there to see what Diego would do. He should have finished the job at hand and made the deal with you, but he didn't. So predictable. No checking. No following protocol. Only worried about his porn and his own sick fantasies. Dickhead."

Montego had apparently been quiet long enough. "I came to town early to take back Diego's business interests. Once you were gone, we'd planned to tell Diego that you were some UC Fed—"

"I'm not an undercover Fed!" Zak wasn't lying. The Organization was not directly linked to the Feds. They might do each other favors on occasion, but nothing was ever official or in writing. The Organization had its own interests and its own private payroll courtesy of a secret benefactor.

"We know." Ernesto shrugged and cleared his throat. "Your part was to be a lesson to the others in the group. Once you hit the ground, Diego was going down next. The others still in the group needed immediate leadership, which I planned to provide."

Zak nodded. "Why don't you take over, Julio?"

Julio walked closer. "Because those Fed fuckers watch me. My father's rep will always hang over my head. Had to be Ernesto. Teach the others about what carelessness will get you, and how we plan to run things from now on."

"What makes Ernesto so trustworthy?" Zak asked.

"History. I was very good friends with Julio's father back when things started. That relationship passed on to Diego when Julio's father went to prison."

"Yeah. But then he became a low-rent wheeler dealer, trading all sorts of shit this group never should have handled," Julio said. "Traditions were let go or abandoned. Plus, he didn't pay enough attention to who the fuck came into the fold. I mean, even though I was the one who stood up for you, he should have checked you out himself. But he didn't. Slacker. He had to go."

Ernesto spoke up again. "Then I did the same thing. I vouched for someone and Diego didn't bother to check and see who he was, just took it on faith that the man I recommended was vetted." He rendered what could only be the most sinister laugh Zak had ever heard. "In fact, I have no idea who he is. Maybe he's on the up and up, maybe he isn't. Diego didn't check, so now he's got to die, too."

Fuck. Miles was officially late now. Where was he?

Zak moved a quarter of a step closer to one of Montego's goons. The guy was totally wrapped up in the drama. If Zak could just get close enough, he could grab the guy's gun, take out the other guard and grab hold of the situation.

"So the guy I'm supposed to be sharing this business deal with is out already?" Zak asked, mostly wanting to be certain Julio or Montego hadn't already buried Miles out behind the warehouse somewhere.

"Technically there isn't a deal at all." Julio looked at his watch. "And he's late anyway. What's up with your boy, Ernesto?"

"He'll be here."

"Do you trust him?"

Both Montego and Julio said at the same time, "No."

Zak asked, "Why are we waiting then?"

Julio grinned. "He's bringing the other half of the money."

Montego shrugged. "Once we have the cash, then you're both dead, and we're out of here."

Demarco started to struggle up to a sitting position but couldn't do it. "How dare you treat me this way? I made shit-tons more money than your father ever managed. Me! I did that."

Julio whipped his gun up, but Brooke screamed. "No! Please don't kill him." She ran to Demarco, dropped to her knees and draped herself over his prone body. "I love you. I'm sorry. I can't do this anymore."

Montego snagged the gun from one of his men, leaving him unarmed. Zak side-stepped quickly to get closer to the other goon.

"Brooke. What are you doing?"

Her mascara streaked eyes met Montego's cold stare. "I love him."

"What about us?"

"I hate you. I've hated you forever. You are the worst, Ernesto! Diego promised me we'd be together once you finished this deal."

The goon with the remaining weapon dipped his arm and Zak moved in. He shot an elbow into the guy's throat and he folded like a lawn chair in a high wind.

Zak grabbed his gun and leveled it at Julio as he kicked the gun easily out of Montego's hand.

Julio tried to take aim at Zak. Zak fired.

"Fucker!" Julio dropped the gun. He'd only been shot in the bicep, but he fell to his knees like something vital had been hit.

Zak marched forward and put the barrel to Julio's head. "Don't move." He noted that if Julio stretched, he could have grabbed a gun from one of Demarco's fallen men, but he didn't. Even so, he kicked the nearest gun well out of his reach. Julio frowned, still clutching his arm.

"Kaitlin," Zak said. "Get out, right now."

She didn't move, looking at the entire scene a bit like a cute deer in the headlights.

They all listened to the sound of another vehicle crunching over the gravel lot beside the warehouse. Doors slammed and someone entered the building. Zak had never been so glad to see Miles, duffel bag in hand and a very surprised-looking guy in tow, presumably Nate the product testing guy.

"What in the world are you doing?" Miles asked, staring around at the tableau of dead goons, a pretty blonde draped over a bleeding Demarco, a bewildered Kaitlin and Zak holding the not-dead Julio, annoying Montego and more henchmen at bay with one gun.

Zak motioned at Miles and his companion. "Drop your bag. Guns on the floor."

"Chill out, dude."

"They were going to kill us and take our money, take the product and even kill Diego, too."

"What the fuck?"

"Until you got here I was thinking about my next steps. You got any thoughts?"

"Where's the product?"

Zak gestured to the table Montego had been leaning

192

against. "Over there maybe, but I'm not certain they even brought anything. This was a bogus meeting meant to teach Diego a lesson. We were used."

"The hell you say." Miles sent Nate over to check out the briefcase on the table. He also pulled a weapon and pointed it in the general direction of Montego, Julio and Demarco, still cuddling with Brooke. All three men looked supremely unhappy.

Miles said, "Maybe we'll just take the product and our money."

"Fine by me," Zak said.

Nate sounded excited when he said, "These are the real deal. The flash drives are legit." Inside the briefcase was a tray filled with row after row of high-end flash drives. If the intel could be believed, which Zak had some doubts about, each offered access to various security systems across the nation.

Miles said, "Excellent. Let's round them up and go."

Before anyone could move, several approaching vehicles and sirens could be heard. Seconds later, the staccato sound of a platoon of footsteps echoed through the rafters of the warehouse.

Then the shouting began. The police dashed forward, guns drawn and a party pack of assorted law enforcement guys at their heels. No one looked more surprised than Montego or Julio to see their meeting compromised.

Zak, Miles and Nate all went to their knees, surrendered their weapons and got arrested with the pack.

Brooke was physically lifted from Demarco when the ambulance arrived to take him. He was handcuffed to the gurney. Brooke screamed obscenities at the paramedics and really anyone within range of her loud voice, until she was also removed.

Kaitlin looked relieved when the police showed up,

and immediately forlorn when Zak was disarmed and handcuffed like all the others. For some reason, the cops were treating her like a victim instead of a suspect, and hadn't cuffed her. He saw her arguing with various officers and pointing at him, but they had their orders. Zak was a bad boy criminal and he was going to jail. She was led outside the warehouse. He lost track of her in the chaos of being shoved in the back of a police transport van. It was about to be a long night.

Zak took solace in the fact that at least they'd had a final moment to straighten out their disagreement from breakfast. Things had worked out, all things considered.

The arrest was all part of protecting the identities he and Miles had cultivated. Nothing helped with that better than being hauled off in the paddy wagon. They even had Kaitlin as an additional witness to Julio, Montego and Demarco's dealings. He likely wouldn't even be released from this fake detention until morning.

It wasn't until later that Zak learned the saddlebags were wired. That was how Miles knew to come when he did, and how the cops had been forewarned to handle Kaitlin carefully. Everything they'd said in the warehouse was evidence and further charges were being collected to ensure that Demarco's former group of criminals would be totally shut down in the area. Julio and Montego's arrests were a welcome bonus, and the two were facing numerous charges of their own.

The morning after their faux arrests, Zak had been removed from his cell and put in a private conference room with Miles when a local law enforcement officer entered. "Langston, there's someone here to bail you out. What would you like me to tell her?"

Miles grinned. "Is her name Kaitlin, by chance?"

The officer nodded and smiled. "Want me to send her on her way?"

Miles looked at Zak. "Go talk to her. You know you

want to. She saved your life, after all, chasing after you the way she did that first night."

"Oh, you heard that, did you?"

"I heard everything. Including your lame proposal and her fear-induced answer." Miles gave him a stern look. "What are you going to do about that now that you've both survived?"

Zak ignored his question. "So am I free or still awaiting trial?"

"Tell her you've agreed to a deal with no jail time. You can even go home with her tonight if you want, but don't forget you're leaving the area. Very soon."

"Right." Zak wasn't certain seeing Kaitlin again was a good idea, but was foolishly happy he'd be able to speak to her alone one last time.

Zak detoured to collect the personal things that had been taken when he was processed like the others, and left through prisoner release to the hallway where Kaitlin waited.

She launched herself into his arms, which closed tightly around her without any conscious order from his brain. "I'm free. Let's go."

"What happened?"

"I made a deal for no jail time."

"Good." But there was a hint of disapproval. Zak desperately wished he could tell her the truth. Too bad she wasn't already his wife. He looked up and saw a sign that made him grin. Because it definitely was *a sign*.

"How's your level of faith in me right now?"

"Bruised." She followed his gaze, and shock filled her expression. Her eyes met his.

"So, will you hang on with me for just a little bit longer?"

Her sudden smile followed by her nod made his heart swell. She tightened her grip on his arm.

Zak hustled her down the hallway toward a place

where they'd both need to have confidence in each other.

Kaitlin gathered her courage and didn't stop to analyze a thing. Going purely on faith, she said to the assembled few, "I do."

Less than an hour ago, she had watched Zak stare at a sign that said Marriage Licenses like he'd just solved all his problems.

The Justice of the Peace said, "I now pronounce you man and wife. You may kiss your bride."

Zak leaned in, kissed her like nobody's business to the cheers of the two witnesses and the other assembled couples getting married this morning.

"My place or yours, Mrs. Langston," Zak said as they skipped down the courthouse steps.

A nervous laugh escaped. "I'm still getting used to being Mrs. Langston instead of Mrs. Thornton. And I don't care where we go, but before we fall into bed, I want you to explain a few things."

"Of course. Now that you're my wife, I can tell you exactly a few things, Mrs. Langston."

Zak did a little explaining and then a lot of taking her to previously unreached heights of pleasure before coming up for air.

As they drowsed together under the sheets, Kaitlin thought how happy she was to have thrown caution to the wind and trusted her heart. Her new husband wasn't a criminal at all. She had a lot to learn about him, the real him, but the most important thing was that he wasn't a felon. He couldn't share mission details, of course, but she didn't care. She'd married a man she was desperately in love with who'd saved her life in more ways than one.

Zak didn't agree.

"The truth is, baby, I was just a bad boy in big trouble until I met you," he said with a laugh.

As he showed her, again, how good a bad boy could be, she sank her nails into his amazing ass and cried out his name. No more peeking through the curtains for virginal little Kaitlin.

From now on she was Zak Langston's woman.

EPILOGUE

Lush, humid air surrounded Zak as he entered the seven-digit keypad code for the house his parents owned in Key West. He hoped they hadn't changed it since the last time he was here. A quiet snick and the back door next to the kitchen unlocked. He turned the handle and pushed the door open. A rush of cool air blasted him in the face.

Bless his sweet mother. She always kept the thermostat set at seventy-two degrees. Like walking out of a sauna and into a refrigerator. Zak was excited to be here and hoped all of his brothers had made it to the biannual gathering.

"Is anyone here?" Kaitlin asked.

He pulled her inside by their clasped hands and closed the door. "Probably. And if not now, soon. Quite a few family members will descend on this house."

"Hard to blame them," Kaitlin said, looking around. "It's a nice place. How often does your family meet here?"

"Twice a year. My parents own it, but rent it out except for the last two weeks of May and October. They reserve that for family. There's an open invitation to any of us boys who can get here. We lounge by the pool, drink beer and catch up on the life and times of whoever makes it."

"How long since you've visited?" Her voice trembled a bit despite the simplicity of her question. He knew why she was nervous.

"I've missed the last two times. Don't worry. They'll be glad I showed up."

She didn't look convinced. "What if they aren't glad that *I* showed up?"

He cupped the side of her face and pressed a reassuring kiss to her lips. "Oh, please. My family, especially my mother, will be delighted. Trust me."

They'd come to Florida all the way from Arizona, enduring not one but two lengthy layovers along the way. It had been five days since they'd exchanged their vows in front of the Justice of the Peace. Zak figured a delayed honeymoon in Key West to announce their marriage was a good plan. Kaitlin was not as confident.

His brother Deke was the lone member of his family who had gotten the surprise news and only because Deke's last job had taken him to Arizona. Zak was looking forward to kicking back in Arizona with his new wife while they waited for Kaitlin's contract to end in four months. The Organization had given him honeymoon leave for as long as he wanted it.

"I'm not so sure," Kaitlin said. "My mother was displeased, as you well know."

"Well, I suspect it's different with daughters and mothers rather than sons and mothers. My mom had given up hope of any of us ever marrying, so she's probably going to squeeze you until bones break. Besides, I think your mom and stepdad are more upset about Brooke being in trouble than you eloping with me."

"I'd say it's a toss-up, but I'm trying to keep a good attitude."

"That's my girl. Or rather, *my woman*."

She sighed rather dramatically. "Before we got married, you used to call me baby. Is the honeymoon over already?"

Zak laughed. "So what you're saying is you want the bad boy back."

Someone pushed the swinging door to the kitchen open, intruding on their laughter.

"Zak, is that you?" A grin spread across his mother's face as soon as she saw him.

"Hi, Mom." Zak folded his mother into an exuberant hug.

She squeezed him tight. "I'm so glad you made it this time. Your father will be, too. You know him. He's just fiddling with the car."

They broke apart and Zak immediately turned to his wife. "Mom, I'd like you to meet Kaitlin."

His mother smiled and hugged her, like he knew she would. "Welcome to the madness of our biannual gatherings."

"Thanks, I'm happy to be here."

Maura Langston had lived in a household with massive levels of testosterone for years, and maybe because of that she'd developed hawkeyed skills a spy would be proud of. Grabbing Kaitlin's left hand, she examined the wedding ring and sucked in a shocked breath. "This is your *wife*, Zak?"

Zak nodded, locking gazes with Kaitlin, who was clearly struggling to keep her smile. "We eloped five days ago."

His mother squealed in joy and hugged Kaitlin so tight, Zak thought he did hear a rib crack. His mother was making happy noises between tears and a babble of conversation. Kaitlin finally seemed to accept her acceptance. She stopped looking so anxious and embraced the older woman wholeheartedly in return.

The two most important women in his life finally finished hugging, but his mother kept a hand on Kaitlin's shoulder like she would disappear in a puff of smoke if she didn't keep a tactile connection. "Well, there's no two ways about it. We'll have to have a celebration feast tonight."

"Oh. Don't go to any trouble," Kaitlin said.

His mother laughed. "It's no trouble, honey. The truth is, with five adult boys to feed, every night is a feast whether we have something to celebrate or not."

"Well, I'm happy to help you cook."

His mother sniffed and teared up. "And you cook, too? That's just so wonderful."

Jack Langston strolled into the kitchen.

"Hey, Dad."

"Zak! Good to see you, son." The older man clapped him on the back once and glanced over at Kaitlin. "What do we have here?"

"Jack, great news! This is *Kaitlin*, Zak's *wife*. Can you believe it?"

His father looked surprised for about a second and a half. Then he laughed and slapped Zak on the back again. He hugged Kaitlin. "Welcome to the family. It's a zoo most of the time, but a fun one."

Jack put one arm around Kaitlin and the other around his wife. "Has she started in on you about grandchildren yet?"

"Dad!"

"Jack!" his mother said at the same time. "They've only been married five minutes. Let's give them a couple months, and then we can start sending e-mail reminders."

His parents led Kaitlin out of the kitchen on a tour of the house. Zak was about to follow when he heard someone outside pushing the buttons on the keypad. The door unlocked and Deke came in.

"Hey. Where's your wife? You didn't lose her already, did you?"

"No, I didn't lose her already. Mom and Dad are showing her the house."

Deke grinned. "How did they take the news?"

"Surprisingly well, actually. I think they'd trade me for her in a second."

"Good for you. I can't wait to meet her. Is anyone else here?"

"Not that I know of, but I haven't made it out of the kitchen yet. I'd better go find Kaitlin. They brought up grandchildren before they walked out."

"You knew that was coming."

Zak shrugged and grinned. "Yeah." He'd never spent much time thinking about children. Like marriage, it was always something he planned to do someday. With a wedding band on his finger, someday had arrived.

Deke punched him in the arm for no discernable reason, because that's what brothers do.

Zak paused in the doorway. "Be nice to me or I'll tell Mom and Dad you knew about the wedding and didn't tell them."

"That's harsh, bro." Deke followed him into the next room.

Zak punched his brother solidly in the shoulder to return the first strike, happy to be back with his family and ready to have a honeymoon with Kaitlin.

Who knew? There might be grandchildren on the way sooner rather than later, if this honeymoon in paradise went well. He was certainly willing to do his part as often as his darling wife desired.

THE END

COMING SOON

BOUNCER
BAD BOYS IN BIG TROUBLE 2

BODYGUARD
BAD BOYS IN BIG TROUBLE 3

Excerpt from

Undercover DEA Agent Reece Langston is used to women coming on to him in his role as a bouncer at the city's hottest club. None of them tempt him to break his own rules of non-engagement—until FBI Agent Jessica Hayes makes him a sexy offer he can't refuse.

PROLOGUE

Saturday night – Joe's Bar

"What do you mean you've never had sex before?" The utter surprise in Kelli Baker's tone was second only to the volume at which she shouted the inflammatory information.

Jessica Hayes sent her soon-to-be-*ex*-best friend a horrified look. Speechless, she promptly lowered her head in abject shame, afraid to look around and see who might have heard the notification to the world of her virginal status. The trendy upscale bar they were in was quiet enough that voices could definitely carry well outside of their private two person circle.

Knowing Kelli as she did and that her friend would continue chattering until stopped, Jessica regrouped quickly and snapped, "Could you say that a little louder? I don't think the single desperate men of Outer Mongolia heard you."

Kelli glanced over one shoulder quickly and promptly touched Jessica's hand in apology. "Well, I'm sorry, but I mean, damn, girlfriend! When you said you *really* needed to get laid I didn't realize we were talking about the premier event. I almost brought a guy with me tonight, but he had to work. So how did you make it to your advanced age without bumping uglies with a guy?"

"Four older brothers and a small Midwestern town." Jessica took a sip of her club soda with lime and the memories of her high school years invaded her thoughts.

The high school boys of Cornelia, Missouri were all cowards. No guy would ever ask her out for fear of retribution. Her shortest brother was six foot two, damn it. A mother bear seemed neglectful in comparison to her brothers and the way they protected her from the advances of any male in a three county radius, a skill they learned well from their father.

Even now she couldn't visit home without all the eligible bachelors between the ages of eighteen and eighty cowering away from her in fear.

"You don't say. Sounds like the title of a bad TV movie of the week."

"Yeah, that's my love life—a bad TV movie of the week broadcast on cable at two in the morning. It isn't as if I haven't tried, you know. I got close a couple of times, but in retrospect I was far too picky."

"Define close," Kelli said, twirling her drink straw around the ice in the bottom of her nearly empty glass.

"My second year of college."

"Do tell."

"He was a sports media major. Deep voice. Sexy deep-blue eyes. He stared at me in the cafeteria for a month before finally asking me out."

"So why didn't you do him?"

"I tried. We went to a pledge week frat party at his fraternity house, where he managed to get rip-roaring drunk in record time. He led me, staggering all the way, to his room. We had to kick out another couple and he cleared most of the coats off the bed before feeling me up a couple times and then ejaculating on the sleeve of one unlucky guest's Burberry jacket."

"Eew. That's just nasty."

"Oh, I'm so sorry to offend your delicate sensibilities. It was a frat party. Everyone knows you take your chances if you leave coats and stuff laying around in any of the bedrooms. That was karma, pure and simple."

"So you didn't even get anything out of the near exchange of bodily fluids?"

"Not really. I got up and left, but quite a few people saw me leave his bedroom. Frat Boy apparently thought he did the deed, so he washed his hands of me directly afterwards and considered the conquest done. On Monday he started staring at a freshman with big boobs and ignored me completely. I was so embarrassed. It took me a year and a half to get up enough nerve to try again."

Kelli shook her head. "He's the one who should have been embarrassed. I wish I'd been around back then to get you back up on the horse." She took a long sip, finished her drink and gestured at the busy bartender to prepare another. "As a matter of fact, if you'd mentioned I was dealing with virgin territory tonight, I would have selected a different place. Hell, I would have hand-picked someone special to take care of you."

The thought of Kelli explaining to *someone special* how her friend needed to be de-virginized made Jessica wish she'd ordered tequila tonight instead of club soda to numb the humiliation.

"Great. Or I could just schedule an appointment with my gynecologist and have it done surgically. Maybe she could light a candle for atmosphere."

"No way. Don't do that. What about all those hunky guys with guns where you work? Surely there are possibilities there, right?"

"No. I never want to date anyone from law enforcement, and especially not anyone I work with."

"Why not?"

"Too weird to have slept with someone and then work with them, knowing what they look like naked. Besides, what if it didn't work out? Too much drama. So no, law enforcement guys are not an option. Move on."

"Fine. Then leave it to me. I'll pick someone nice, someone you won't ever see again, and most especially a guy who knows what he's doing without any guilt-filled strings attached."

"So a total stranger you know firsthand is sexually amazing? That man surely doesn't exist or you'd already have him chained to your bed. I don't need you to find anyone for me. I especially don't want someone you've been with."

"Are you sure? I know a guy or two who would volunteer in an emergency." Kelli smiled. "This seems like an emergency to me."

"Well, it's not. And really? Men you've used up and thrown away? No, thank you very much."

"It's not like that. The men I have in mind didn't work for me in other ways. Or I didn't work for them, but we remained friends. It can be done."

"So you say. Still, I'm not looking for a friend of yours to deflower me."

"I would have volunteered," said a sleazy voice from over Jessica's shoulder. A voice that sent a shard of panic to her heart. A voice she recognized from work.

Damn it all to hell.

Jessica swiveled on her bar stool, coming face-to-face Agent Neil Wiley, resident dick and infamous idiotic office lothario. After keeping a low profile these past several months since moving here from her Midwestern hometown after FBI training, Neil—also known as the bastard of the second floor—had just learned her deepest secret.

Jessica tried not to gnash her teeth in frustration. Given Neil's proclivity to gossip, she knew by Monday morning the entire FBI building would be apprised of her limited sexual expertise. Or worse, he'd hound her about it privately until she shot out his kneecaps in annoyance. Then again, the paperwork involved in firing her service weapon might just be worth it in this case.

She shouldn't care about Neil, but it was hard enough to make friends, especially male friends, in a new city without having a cloud of virginity smack dab over her head.

"As a matter of fact, I'll volunteer right now. Want to go to your place or mine so I can pop your cherry, Agent Hayes?" he asked and bit into a green olive from his martini.

Chapter 1

Well after midnight on a lonely street

Reece Langston fell in love with her delicious heart-shaped ass first, because that was the first part he saw. The goddess was bent over rummaging around the open trunk of her car, which sported a flat tire, muttering curses as clanking ensued.

"...stupid frickin'...ah ha! There you are!"

When she straightened and emerged clutching a tire iron in one fisted hand, he got his first look at the angelic face that went with that lovely derriere. She simply took his breath away. She was a blonde. He loved blondes. Her hair fell to her shoulders in waves. She was tall, but not overly so. She had long shapely legs attached to that gorgeous butt, and he easily pictured them wrapped around his naked, sweaty waist as he thrust endlessly... *Calm down*, he told himself.

A ferocious urge stirred in his loins, the likes of which made him look down at his own crotch in wonder. He waited, almost expecting to see his cock burst through the zipper of his jeans to take a closer look at the delectable instigator of the rampant excitement pervading the space below his belt.

It had been so long.

Reece glanced back up in time to see her squat beside the rear passenger-side tire, thrusting her ass out in his direction again. The slacks she wore hugged her lower half nicely. He had to close his eyes because the visual overwhelmed him, and wondered how best to convince the angel before him they were destined to be together.

Tonight. Now. Was her back seat big enough for the both of them?

Another glance at his mystery future lover as she applied the tire iron to the unseen jack under her car made him smile. He thought of an opening line to break the ice.

"You're doing it wrong," he told her in an overloud tone. She startled, almost lost her balance, and shot him an evil glare over one slim shoulder. He cursed his long deprived reptilian libido, realizing it was foolish to sneak up on a woman fixing a flat tire at night on a deserted street. He was lucky she hadn't just shot him through the heart, or worse, whipped out her pepper spray keychain to blind him. He'd volunteer to be gut shot before ever being sprayed with that evil shit again.

"Oh, am I?" Her belligerent tone was not a surprise. No gun came forth to add meaning to her justified attitude. Reece was glad she wasn't a frail little flower.

He nodded, shaping an innocent smile on his lips. "I'm afraid so."

She stood and put one hand on her hip. "I know you don't know this about me, since we're strangers and all, but I've changed a flat tire before, so you can run along." She glanced back to her task, muttering, "I'm not *either* doing it wrong."

He tilted his head to one side and smiled at her frustrated expression. Crossing his arms, he leaned against the light pole behind him and prepared to watch the show.

Her narrowed gaze pierced his face. "What do you think you're doing?"

"I want to watch and learn, oh great experienced tire changer."

"Why? Need some pointers?" One beautiful brow lifted in challenge.

He laughed. "No. I want to watch and see how you loosen the lug nuts on that flat tire once your car is jacked up all the way in the air. So please, do carry on." He gestured for her to continue.

She turned back to the tire and muttered another whispered curse, "...stupid frickin' lug nuts..." She twisted back with an angry expression, which quickly softened into a heart-melting grin. "Well, I guess you've got me there."

"I'd be happy to help you change that tire. Or ridicule you further while you do it. Lady's choice."

She laughed, picked up the cross-shaped four-way lug wrench, and held it out to him. He leaned up from the post, approached her slowly and took it. He hoped she didn't look down just yet. His cock had reacted fervently and swelled outward another inch in response to the scent of her when he stepped into her personal space to grab the tool. Cursing his self-imposed sexual drought, Reece took a step past her and noticed she let him brush very close without stepping out of the way.

She smelled like sex. Or did everything smell like sex because he wanted her so badly?

"I'll let you get your hands dirty." Her golden blond hair, which brushed her shoulders in curly waves, framed an oval face. Now that he was closer, he saw the color of her eyes. Sea green. Or maybe a color like dew-kissed grass.

I am a total sap. A big, horny, sappy goof.

She was interested in him, too. She stared, most particularly at *his* ass when she thought he wasn't looking. He didn't mind. Turnabout was fair play. She was the perfect height. Tall enough that her head would line up with his shoulders if they hugged, short enough to be able to wear spike heels if they ever went dancing.

He squatted down to change her tire and completed the task in record time. All the while he tried to figure out a way to entice her up to his apartment. He lived across the street and just down the block. Reece wasn't usually such a letch with strange women, but she stirred something deeply important within him, something he'd missed.

Plus, she gave him a record-breaking hard-on. After a night of getting fake hit-on for the sole purpose of gaining entrance into his club, Reece was ready for the interest of someone who didn't want anything from him but company or perhaps, better yet, pleasure.

He glanced at his apartment building, wondering what he could say to get her to accompany him inside. His car was parked in a garage a block away. He'd been on his way home after a long night at work when she had distracted him. Her and her shapely, sexy ass. He kicked the release on the jack, lowered the car to the ground, tightened the final lug nut in place on the replacement tire, and stood with the intention of being charming.

"Are you married?" she asked before he could say a word. She stepped directly into his personal space. He inhaled, taking in and memorizing her lovely scent.

"No. Are you?" He breathed in her unique fragrance once more. This time he wasn't as circumspect. The dance of love had begun. She was considering him, he could tell. Otherwise, why would it matter if he had a wife?

"Nope." Her voice lowered to a husky tone with that

single-word answer. She reached out as she spoke and smoothed the front of his jacket with her palm. "I've never even been engaged." The sensation of her touch sent a pulse of desire straight to his balls.

"Good." He was glad he still had the ability to speak without simply grunting a response. He reached up and trapped her hand on his chest, caressing her soft skin with his thumb.

"Is it good?" She took another step closer. Her breasts brushed his upper torso. Her hips rested against his. She couldn't possibly miss his cock trying its best to stand at attention to impress her.

He raised his free hand to tuck a stray lock of her soft hair behind her ear and whispered, "It will be." He genuinely hoped they were having the same conversation. He was talking about sweaty, satisfying sex.

"Do you promise?" Her head tilted, eyes seeking his, and he knew she certainly couldn't miss the beast in his pants throbbing forward in response, promising all good things to come if she'd only accompany him to his apartment.

"I do." Reece used his best convincing voice to add, "I know you don't know this about me, since we're strangers and all, but I—" The sudden connection of her seductive mouth pressing to his cut off whatever he was about to say, which he couldn't remember anyway because her tongue licked his bottom lip and slipped inside to caress gently about.

For his part, he dragged her up into his arms. She slanted her mouth across his to deepen this, their first intoxicating kiss. Perfection.

"Do you live close?" she asked, breaking the luscious connection just long enough to ask the question before planting her mouth on his again. One of her hands slid around to brush the stubble at the nape of his neck. He kept his hair very closely cropped. As a bouncer for a premier club, it completed his dangerous bad-assed look. He was glad she wasn't deterred in any way by his appearance. Some women told him they found him frightening, right before they got a glint in their eye that said they were willing to do *anything* to get inside his club.

He tightened his grasp around her and twisted them until he pressed her against the car. He slid a hand down her back, fingertips feeling their way to cup her lovely ass. He pressed her more firmly into his groin, which was already grinding against her rhythmically. His cock stiffened and pulsed in anticipation, gearing up to do the deed here and now on the street corner.

A glimpse of sanity intruded. Perhaps he shouldn't treat her like a prostitute. She felt incredibly good...but perhaps he should make sure she *wasn't* a prostitute.

He broke from the kiss. "Yes. I live very close. What's your name?"

Her panicked look startled him as her whole body stiffened. "No names!"

"What?"

She took a deep breath, pushed it out slowly, and melted back into him. "No names," she repeated softly. "Can't this just be a private, mutually beneficial evening without an exchange of detailed information?"

"Sure. Okay. No names. How about if I call you Smith? Or did you want to be Jones?" This was an interesting conundrum. The name he would have given her was Mark Reece. It was the undercover name he used for his current job as a bouncer. He wondered what *she* was hiding from.

"Gentleman's choice." She grabbed a handful of his ass and brought him close. "I just want to get naked with you. Is that too bold of me?"

"No. But aren't you worried? I mean, I *am* a stranger

and all." *And I'm scary looking to some women, but not to you, apparently.*

"Are you going to hurt me?" She flashed a grin and he wanted to eat her up one bite at a time.

Amused, he said, "No." He was going to make sweet love to her until they were both sweaty, breathing hard and completely satisfied. "I was about to assure you that I'd never let any harm come to you."

"That's what I thought. Besides, I can take care of myself. Also, I have a good feeling about you, Jones."

"What are you basing your feeling on?" He nudged her with his hips, allowing his cock to introduce itself yet again, like the unruly beast hadn't already been dry humping her for the last several minutes in blatant overture.

"You smell nice, you have a sense of humor, and you did me a huge favor changing that tire. But mostly, I've been a long time without the comfort of a man. I believe you're worth taking a chance on." She nudged back and he had to close his eyes a moment. This whole situation smacked of *setup*.

Then why wasn't he getting that tingly feeling in his belly that things weren't what they seemed?

Maybe she really *was* looking for a quick and easy hookup with no strings attached. He shouldn't let his little head dictate this evening. What was she after? Was this no-names thing a ploy?

"So are you looking for a new boyfriend or a sugar daddy or something and just reeling me in for a later changeup?"

Her eyes widened in surprise. "No. I swear. I'm only looking for an anonymous Mr. Right Now, not a forever commitment. I don't want a permanent fixture in my life, just some sex tonight. Okay?"

"Good enough, Smith. I live across the street." He nodded in the direction of his building.

"Perfect. Let's go, Jones."

Reece couldn't believe his good fortune. He put her tools and flat tire in her trunk as his blood sang with delectable sexual possibilities. Closing the trunk soundly, he grabbed her hand. He couldn't decide what to do with her first. Fuck her in the vestibule of his apartment building before she changed her mind? This from the lusty beast in his pants.

No, not my style. At least find a soft surface. His bed had a very soft surface, and he should taste her first. Tasting her would probably send him over the edge before he even got his cock inside of her body, but what a way to go.

Yes, he would whisk her up to his apartment and taste her first. Always a popular appetizer to make the rest of the night last longer. Besides, he'd been too long without the comfort of a woman to be good enough his first round through.

Being undercover for so long gave him limited options with regard to any sort of love life. This arrangement of two sexually deprived people on a path to an anonymous, lust-filled night of passion worked perfectly if he never wanted to see her again.

Reece inhaled her delectable fragrance once more, glanced at the top of her blonde head and wondered if one night would be enough to quench his already sizable thirst for her.

Jessica was about to get laid. *Hallelujah!* The delicious stranger who had so expertly changed her tire also set off her sexy man pheromone warning system the minute he stepped into sensory range. He was tall and muscular with dark hair and chocolate-brown eyes. He had casual clothing under a nice leather jacket, not like a scruffy biker one. He was a big guy, imposing because of his height, but she didn't feel the least uncomfortable in his presence. He was engaging, mesmerizing, completely unfamiliar and she was falling in lust with him.

She watched his hands as he removed the tire from her car and enviously wished those large, square-shaped fingers caressed her body instead of her steel-belted radial. She wanted him to skip the tire change and work on her. Her head had been filled with questions. Would he have sex with her? Was he the one? Wasn't he already the perfect choice to rid her of her virginal status issues?

As he worked, she developed a plan. If she could talk this delectable stranger into a quick round of take-me-tonight sex, then when she went back to work on Monday, she'd no longer be a virgin.

ABOUT THE AUTHOR

Fiona Roarke lives a quiet life with the exception of the characters and stories roaming around in her head. She writes about sexy alpha heroes, using them to launch her series, *Bad Boys in Big Trouble*.

Find Fiona Online:

www.FionaRoarke.com

www.facebook.com/FionaRoarke

Printed in Great Britain
by Amazon

86169997R00132